You Will

Molly Garcia

Contents

1.

2.

3.

4.

5.

6.

7.

8.

9.
10.
11.
12.
13.
14.
15.
16.

Acknowledgements

Iowe quite a few thank-yous!

Firstly, Amanda Elliott who is hugely supportive and does a lot of behind-the-scenes help for me.

Hailey Drewes-Montney who proofread this book and helped me spot those pesky grammar issues!

Grant Love who is the most amazing narrator out there, if you haven't already I strongly suggest you try anything that he's produced.

Sooz Simpson – aka Katherine Black – a fantastic author in her own right. I've read so many of her books and keep on looking forward to the next ones! If you haven't read one yet then you don't know what you're missing. Not only is Sooz an author, but she's also one of the most supportive, kind, and thoughtful people that I've ever met. She does a huge amount for other indie authors through her FaceBook group (BBE – Best Book Editors: Authors, readers welcome) and we all appreciate it very much.

Dawn Angels - who also runs a supportive group on FaceBook (Psychological Thriller Authors and Readers Unite)

I'd also like to mention another group – Psychological Thriller Readers – all the admin and members are brilliant, but I'd like to mention Chris Colmenero specifically. She's also an indie author and having read two of her books would recommend any thriller fans give her a try.

I also have a fabulous team behind me:

Rhonda Lynn Bobbit, Angie Reuter, JoAnn WX, Ash Adam, Legacy Bookish, and Corina Prince.

Without you guys I think I'd have given up on everything quite a few times! You bolster me up, help spread the word about my books, and cheer me on. Thank you doesn't really seem enough to describe how grateful I am.

This book is dedicated to my partner Darren who played my muse when I struggled to put my ideas together.

Prologue

15TH FEBRUARY 2024

DCI Kevin Greggs rubbed his hands together as though he was cold. He fixed a stern look at the man sitting opposite him in the interview room.

"I'm not a great believer in coincidence, Mr Folder. Maybe it's all these years in the police force that's made me so cynical, but I just can't swallow a coincidence this big."

The man opposite swallowed hard. He opened his mouth to speak, but his lawyer dug her elbow into her client's arm.

"Mr Folder, just a reminder of your right to silence."

Brett Folder winced and closed his mouth. DCI Greggs picked up the file in front of him and peeled back the cover as though checking the contents. As he did, the crime scene photos slid out and skittered across the table until they stopped in front of Brett. The colour drained out of his face and he reared back in his chair causing it to scrape across the floor. He hit the wall behind him with a crash and stared at Kevin in horror.

“Why the fuck would you show me those?”

DCI Greggs flicked him a disgusted look as he gathered the photos back up.

“Don’t like looking at your own handy work sir?”

The solicitor shook her head, “That was a cheap trick, Greggs.”

Kevin shrugged, he wasn’t bothered about pissing off the brief, he was, however, interested to see Brett’s extreme response to those photos.

"My client has only just been bereaved and you think it's appropriate to drop graphic photos of her dead body in front of him?"

Clearly, the solicitor was determined to drum the point home for the benefit of the tape, Kevin smirked annoyingly but didn't bother speaking. He shuffled through the photos before lining them all up in date order on the table so they were facing Brett.

"Mr Folder, would you like to comment on any of these photos?"

Brett scooted as far away from the table as he possibly could, he shook his head and then closed his eyes.

"Why are you tormenting me like this? I had nothing to do with any of those deaths."

"Then you're a very unlucky man. A death every Valentine's Day since 2020, and you're asking me to believe it's a coincidence?"

Brett's solicitor was trying to get her client to stay silent, but Brett wasn't going to let that pass without challenge.

"I've got an alibi for each one and you know it. They were ruled accidental deaths, it was terrible and tragic, but why would I kill them? I'm not a psychopath."

Kevin smirked, "I'll leave that diagnosis to a psychiatrist Mr Folder. I'm going to get myself a nice snack and a cup of something hot and wet. I'll leave you and your brief to have a quick chat before we resume this conversation."

DCI Greggs announced the end of the interview to the tape before switching it off and leaving the room. As he closed the door behind him he could already hear Brett's solicitor speaking and he smiled at the nervous tone to her voice.

This time he had Brett Folder bang to rights and they both knew it.

Chapter One

FEBURARY 2020 - RUBY STEVENS

The day passed slowly, Ruby sighed as she tapped her fingernails on the desk and watched the hands on the clock slowly click through the seconds.

"A watched clock doesn't move you know."

Her colleague, Helen, was smiling at her, "I'm guessing you've got a hot Valentine's date with your hot new man to get home to."

Ruby nodded, "I'm meeting him at a flash restaurant for dinner, then it's back to his place…"

She blushed and trailed off as Helen started laughing, "I don't think I need to know any of those details! Sounds serious between you two?"

"I think it might be. He's such a gentleman, and he treats me so well it's amazing. I know it's only been a few months, but when you know, you know."

Helen laughed again, "Very true. When the right one comes along and it feels right, you've got to grasp the moment."

When Ruby gave another glance at the clock her colleague looked around the room before leaning over and whispering, "Why don't you just get off? No one will notice, and it's only half an hour early anyway."

Ruby didn't need telling twice, she gave her friend a grin and grabbed her bag. Waving goodbye she plunged out of the doors and walked briskly up the road. It was bitterly cold, but the first signs that Spring was on its way were all around her. Daffodils waved their yellow heads in the breeze, and the trees were budding with new leaves. It gave Ruby a warm feeling inside to think that this was a new beginning for her as well as for nature.

It'd been a completely chance meeting with Brett, and he'd changed the course of her life. Ruby, recently out of a bad relationship with a man who cheated on her, wasn't keen to meet anyone else. Her best friend wasn't going to let her wallow though, and decided to drag her along to a music gig at a local pub. That's where she'd met Brett. He'd been hanging around and looking as awkward and out of place as she felt. The band wasn't really her cup of tea and she'd just started to wonder how long she'd have to endure it before she could politely excuse herself and go home.

"Is it just me, or do they sound like a badly tuned radio?"

The tall man next to her bent over and yelled his comment in her ear. Ruby nodded, "I'm voting for badly tuned radio."

The man waved his hand toward the bar, "I'm Brett by the way, can I get you a drink? It might help us deal with that racket!"

Ruby smiled and introduced herself, "I'm Ruby, but my friends call me Rubes. Yes please to the drink, can I have a large white wine?"

The evening looked up from that moment onwards. Brett turned out to be fascinating and the rubbish band faded into the background as they chatted and took turns buying each other drinks. At the end of the night, they'd hung on until the landlord was putting away the stools and giving hints about it being time to go. Outside Brett looked awkward again, as though he wasn't quite sure how to say goodnight.

"Can I have your number?"

He'd sounded abrupt and from his blush had realised it too, Ruby tapped her number into his phone and he called her so she had his as well. When Ruby got a text from him first thing the next day she'd known he was interested and it'd grown from there. Their first Christmas and New Year had almost been spoiled when some psycho ex of Brett's had stormed over and poured a drink over her head on New Year's Eve, but over all it was going well.

Her mum still wasn't keen, and she hadn't seen the funny side of the drink-on-the-head incident either.

"What's to say he isn't cheating on her with you? You've only got his word for it that she's the problem. it's early days Rubes, play it safe and don't rush in."

She understood her mum's words of caution, she'd fallen for some right bastards in the past and her mum was understandably worried about her daughter. Ruby knew this was right though, she'd never felt this way about anyone else before and couldn't believe he felt the same way. Take tonight, for the first time a bloke was invested enough to take her somewhere special and make a fuss of her.

Ruby patted her bag, she'd bought him an expensive bottle of the aftershave he liked. She hoped she hadn't gone over the top on the card, at the time it had seemed perfect, but she was starting to worry it was too twee. By now Ruby had arrived at the station. It was starting to get busy and streams of commuters filed through the doors. Joining the crowd she shuffled towards the barriers where she bleeped herself through with her oyster card. Her platform was a bit of a walk and she knew a tube was due in a few minutes. Picking up her pace she weaved around people trying to make it in time.

Almost there, she thought, just as a small boy pulled away from his mum's hand and darted in front of her. The few seconds it took to avoid walking into him cost her the first tube. Ruby heard the whoosh as it sped out of the platform, she slowed down, her shoulders sagging with disappointment.

Determined to get a decent seat on the next one, Ruby crept through the crowds until she reached the painted line that told her not to risk standing any further forward. Ruby craned her neck up the tunnel trying to see if it was coming despite the sign above her head telling her she still had three minutes.

Finally, thought Ruby as she heard the familiar sound of the oncoming train roaring down the tunnel. Hefting her bag strap further up her arm she stepped over the line and leaned forwards to check how far away the train was. The lights were almost upon her and she glanced at the windows to see how full the carriages were. She'd picked standing on the far end of the platform because there was more chance of a seat at the rear of the tube.

The shove from behind came as a complete surprise. Ruby hadn't regained her balance from her peek up the tunnel and she found herself propelled forward with no chance of stopping. She knew she was heading for the edge of the platform and instinctively put out her hands to try and break her fall or find something to clutch onto to stop her falling.

Her hands waved in the air helplessly. it was almost as though she was flying for a moment before the tracks raced up to meet her. Ruby didn't feel the electricity that coursed through her body because by then she was already dead. The oncoming tube plowed into her, bursting her head open like a ripe grape.

DCI Kevin Greggs ducked under the crime scene tape and headed towards the huddle of people at the far end of the platform. Someone had helpfully laid a sheet over the body, but the dark red staining across the material suggested the damage that lay underneath. His DS, Steve Harding, was currently going through the CCTV to work out if it was a tragic accident or suicide. There was always the outlying chance she was pushed, but it was highly unlikely. These cases were most often suicides, but with the rush for trains home and overcrowded stations, Kevin couldn't rule out an accident either.

The forensic pathologist, Nigel Pillsbury, climbed back up onto the platform from the tracks.

"I found a work ID attached to a lanyard around her neck. Ruby Stevens was employed as a support worker and appeared to be on her way home. The fall from the platform alone would've caused significant injuries and that's without her being hit by an oncoming tube and then electrified by the live rails she landed on. As you can imagine the body is in a bit of a state to say the least."

Kevin sighed, "Poor cow. Did you manage to retrieve any other personal possessions?"

Dr Pillsbury handed over an evidence bag containing a mobile phone. "I took the liberty of using the fingerprint technology to open it. We're fortunate it wasn't set to facial recognition considering how she currently looks."

Taking the bag, Kevin glanced at the screen to see a new text message had arrived just before Ruby would've lost signal at the station.

I'm on my way to Bliss now, I know the table isn't booked until 7pm but I can't wait to see you!

He frowned, "What's Bliss when its at home?"

The doctor gave him an eye roll, "Either you're single or too mean to take your significant other to an expensive restaurant. Bliss is the "in" place to eat right now. Very pricey menu, but if you want to impress then that's where you go. It is Valentine's Day, so a good excuse for pushing the boat out."

Kevin knew the doctor was fishing for information about his relationship status, and since he had no intention of making his personal life public knowledge at work, he just ignored the obvious hint.

"Considering it's now gone 7, I'd say we'll find the unfortunate Brett already waiting patiently for his girlfriend and wondering if he's been stood up. I'll get over there with DS Harding and break the bad news."

They'd found Brett seated at a romantic corner table. The candles were lit, the champagne was on ice, and a single rose was placed in a vase in the middle of the table. It was the perfect Valentine's Day setup, and DCI Greggs was about to ruin it.

Mr Folder looked up as they approached, his face hopeful until he saw it was two men standing by his table. Kevin discretely flipped his warrant card and saw Brett's expression change to one of puzzlement.

"I'm not sure what I'm supposed to have done officers, but can't this wait until tomorrow? My girlfriend is about to join me for dinner, she's a bit late, but I expect she got held up at work."

Kevin hated this part of the job. Telling relatives and loved ones that they'd lost someone was never easy.

"I'm so sorry sir, Ruby Stevens was involved in an accident at the station earlier this evening."

Brett was already getting to his feet, "Oh God, is she okay? Can you take me to the hospital to be with her, please? What happened?"

Denial. It was one of the most common reactions. Kevin could see that Brett knew deep down why they were there, but he was still hoping it wasn't true. The last thing he wanted was to tell the man in a busy restaurant so his grief was witnessed by a load of strangers.

"Mr. Folder, could I trouble you to come outside with us for a moment so we can talk more privately?"

Brett nodded, he looked numb as he followed the officers to the door, but before they could leave, the head waiter tapped Kevin on the shoulder.

"We have a private room you can use officer, follow me."

The room turned out to be the staff area, but Kevin was grateful to have access to a place more appropriate for breaking this news. He waited until they were all seated to begin.

"I'm sorry to inform you sir, but Ruby Stevens unfortunately died at the scene of the accident. It looks as though she fell from the platform onto the tracks and was hit by an oncoming tube."

Brett went white as a sheet, "No, you've got the wrong person. It can't be my Ruby. It must be hard to identify her so I expect you've got it wrong."

DCI Greggs passed over Ruby's ID badge in the evidence bag, it was smeared with blood but you could easily see the photo and the name.

"This was around the victim's neck sir."

A cold shiver ran down Kevin's back, a more realistic description would've been "what was left of her neck." It could hardly be called a neck anymore since there was no head attached to it.

Folder's hand shook as he took the ID. He stared at the card for almost a full minute before letting out a howl of pain and slipping from his seat onto the floor. Clutching the ID card to his chest he sobbed, tears streamed down his cheeks and Kevin hovered awkwardly in front of him. He was never quite sure what to do at this point. His natural instinct was to offer comfort, but he wasn't a tactile man given to physically reaching out to strangers so he wasn't sure how to support this wailing man.

"Is there anyone I can call for you sir?"

When Brett nodded, Kevin felt a wave of relief that he could pass the comforting part on to someone else.

"My best friend, Piper Daniels."

Brett fumbled in his pocket until he found his mobile phone, "This is her number, can you call her, please? I don't think I'm able to manage it right now."

DS Harding took the phone and did the honours while Kevin did his best to help Brett back into his chair and offer what verbal comfort he could. The friend couldn't have been far away because it wasn't long until she raced into the room and threw her arms around Brett. Kevin looked away as the man started to sob again loudly. Piper stroked his hair like a mother comforting a small child, before turning to the two officers.

"Do you need anything else from Brett or can I take him home now?"

Kevin couldn't think of anything else to say, and it was with no small amount of relief that he excused himself and Harding.

Outside Steve lit a cigarette, "That was shit wasn't it boss?"

Kevin managed a smile, "The master of understatement as always, Harding. Poor bloke, this is a Valentine's he won't forget in a hurry."

Kevin closed the file on his desk and leaned back in his chair.

The coroner had just come back with his outcome – Accidental Death. The CCTV had been reviewed, any witnesses that had come forward had been interviewed, and Ruby's friends and family spoken to. There were no indications she was suicidal, to the contrary, she'd been the happiest anyone had seen her with her new relationship with Brett Folder. The witnesses hadn't seen anything suspicious, but then they'd been wrapped up in their own journey home. Most hadn't even noticed Ruby until it was too late and she'd fallen off the platform.

The CCTV showed the crowd surging forward as the tube made its way to the platform. Without anything definitive, the coroner had made a judgment that Ruby must've either lost her footing or been accidentally pushed by the crowd of people hurrying to be the first at the doors. She'd stepped over the yellow safety line just before her accident which meant she was too close to the edge. The coroner said he wasn't surprised by the outcome, "People are so desperate to get on the tubes they ignore the safety advice, I'm only surprised it doesn't happen more often."

The only discrepancy that Kevin had found was quickly resolved, and besides, he couldn't say that it would've made any difference to the end result. Brett

Folder's last text to Ruby suggested he was heading to the restaurant as she'd walked onto the platform at 18.30. However, the staff stated that he hadn't arrived until just gone 19.00. When Kevin asked Brett about it, he'd sniffed back his tears to explain.

"I was on my way when I spotted a stain on my shirt and had to turn back to change. I knew I'd still have time to get there before Ruby because she was only just getting her train."

His face had crumpled as he asked, "Oh god, I was concerned about a small mark on my shirt while she was dying."

He'd broken down in huge gasping sobs as his friend Piper glared at the officers, "Don't you think that's enough now?"

Kevin had apologised, there wasn't anything else to say. It all made perfect sense, and the man was clearly devastated. He'd sobbed silently throughout the inquest, clutching his friend Piper's hand as they sat alongside Ruby's parents and sister who were also crying as the accidental death verdict was handed down.

Kevin sighed, it was a horrible tragedy. A woman who'd just found the man she believed to be her life partner slipping on a platform and dying before they could celebrate their first Valentine's Day. Having faced the loss of his own partner three years ago, Kevin knew exactly how it felt to be suddenly bereaved.

He'd lived with Rachel Harman for five years before she was killed in a hit-and-run as she walked home from work one evening. The perpetrator turned out to be a frightened kid who'd taken his parent's car for a joyride. Seeing him sent to juvie hadn't quelled the feelings of bitterness. More families destroyed, was his only thought as he watched the kid's mother sob throughout the trial.

Shaking off the dark thoughts of his past, Kevin pushed the file into the evidence box, put on the lid, and added it to the pile waiting to be taken to the storage facility.

Chapter Two

FEBRUARY 2021 - MANDY FORBES

Mandy Forbes grabbed her mask from the hook by the front door and tucked it into her pocket. In the last almost a year, it'd become second nature to take one with her as it had for countless others across the world. Part of her yearned for a return to normality, leaving the house without thinking about masks and being able to come and go as she pleased. The other part of her couldn't help but thank the pandemic for the gift it had given her.

Last Summer, while out walking in the fresh air, her life had changed forever. She'd got talking to the sad-faced man she'd often seen in the local park while out for her daily exercise. She'd wondered what made him look as though the world was coming to an end, but it wasn't until they got talking that he told her all about it. The poor man had lost his girlfriend to a tragic accident on Valentine's Day. Mandy's heart went out to him, how terrible it must've been. As the pubs started to open and allow customers to sit in the garden they'd started going out for a drink together and things had grown from there. Their first meal had been one of those eat–out -to-help-out things, with Brett joking it was more like "Eat out to Spread Covid about."

When it became obvious that another lockdown was around the corner Brett had impulsively asked Mandy to move in with him.

"I know it's early days, and in normal times we'd be taking this slower, but if we don't do it now we won't see each other hardly at all once there's another lockdown."

Mandy could see the sense in it and hadn't hesitated to agree. She hated her bedsit anyway so she wasn't giving much up. Lockdown had brought home how little access she had to outdoor space and being cooped up in that small room was so depressing. Brett, on the other hand, had a house with a nice little garden. Not that it was the only reason for her moving in, but it did put the cherry on the cake.

It was their first Valentine's Day and of course, they were eating at home because everything was closed down again. Not that Mandy minded, she liked the idea of an intimate meal at home. They'd ended up drinking the bottle of red wine last night, so here was

Mandy popping to the off licence to get another one. She'd left Brett at home prepping the meal and she smiled to herself as she thought about how lovely their evening was going to be.

The street lights cast a dim glow across the pavement, it was cold, damp, and dark, so most people were snuggled up indoors. The shop was a short walk from their house. She walked to the top of the road until she reached the busier street that she needed to cross to get to the shop. Pausing on the kerb to wait until the traffic slowed she was still thinking about her evening when she felt someone take a tight grip on her upper arm. Mandy pulled back instinctively, but all that did was to put her off balance. As she teetered on the kerb she had a moment's hope that she'd be able to stop herself falling. Her heels were just above the pavement's surface and she was standing on just the balls of her feet. Mandy's heart was racing at the near miss. That was all she needed, to have an accident and end up in hospital on Valentine's night. She thought of Brett at home opening the steaks and wondering what was taking her so long.

That was when the person gripping her arm spun her onto the road. Turning her head Mandy realised that the bright lights coming her way belonged to a large lorry.

She didn't have time to scream before it hit her head on.

DCI Greggs was checking through the overnight crime reports when he came across a familiar name. Brett Folder's new partner, Mandy Forbes, had apparently fallen into the path of an oncoming lorry and been killed instantly. What chimed a bell in his head was recalling that Brett's previous girlfriend had also come to a similar end exactly a year ago.

According to the officers who'd broken the news Brett was sitting at home waiting for Mandy to return with a bottle of wine to go with dinner. He was described as being devastated, completely broken up by the news, and Kevin thought back to his own experience with Brett. How much of a coincidence could it be that the man had lost two girlfriends on the exact same day two years on the trot?

Kevin ran Brett through the system to see if he had anything of interest in his past and came across only one interaction with the police previously. An ex-partner by the name of Lily Banks had made an accusation of assault against him. According to the records, she'd then withdrawn the complaint so the case was closed. Lily's original statement claimed that Brett had physically grabbed her upper arm, shaken her violently, and then threatened to kill her. What interested Kevin the most though, were the words he'd used, "I'll make it look like an accident and no one will ever know."

So far this also looked like an unavoidable accident. The pavements were slippery and the kerb was uneven. It wouldn't be surprising that Mandy could've lost her footing and fallen onto the road into the path of an oncoming lorry. The area wasn't covered by CCTV and no one else had been out to witness it. That meant the whole case was based upon supposition and the educated guesswork of the pathologist. There was nothing to suggest it was anything more than it seemed, but Kevin couldn't shake his gut feeling that something was wrong.

A month later Kevin was none the wiser. The coroner had closed the case as an accidental death, and no matter how hard he searched Kevin couldn't find Lily Banks. He'd been hoping to talk to her about Brett Folder and the accusations she'd made against him but she'd vanished without a trace.

Her disappearance increased his suspicions, had she gone underground to avoid being found by her abusive ex? Even worse, had he done something terrible to her that hadn't come to light yet?

Kevin closed his eyes, this was just his imagination running away with him. The case was closed and he had a pile of others waiting for him to focus on. The problem was, he couldn't just ignore a gut feeling. A quick chat with Brett Folder wouldn't go amiss, he thought. He could say he was popping by to offer his condolences and ask if there was anything more he could do.

Decision made he swept up his coat and keys and hurried out of the station. It was now March and whilst it was still chilly, the first signs of Spring were everywhere. At Brett's house, it was a woman who answered and at first Kevin was taken aback. Had he already moved on and found himself someone else? It turned out it was the same woman who'd come to comfort him at the restaurant.

Piper Daniels was reluctant to let Brett speak to her friend.

"He's upset enough as it is without you bringing it all back."

Kevin's apology had melted some of her resistance, but she still watched him like a hawk as he approached her friend.

"Mr Folder, I'm so sorry for your loss. I wanted to share that personally, and ask if you feel we've done everything we could for you."

Brett wiped his eyes, "Yes thank you, officer. It was a tragic accident, and I wouldn't want the driver of the lorry to go through any more than he already has."

The driver had told officers that she'd shot out in front of him without warning. He hadn't had time to apply the brakes or avoid hitting her. The man was devastated and even a ruling of accidental death hadn't stopped him constantly contacting the police to ask if he was going to be arrested.

An awkward silence fell across the room, Brett was still sniffing back tears and his friend, Piper, was shooting looks at the clock on the wall. It was clear she was hinting that his time was up. Kevin wasn't sure how to introduce Lily to the conversation, he just knew he wanted to so he could see the look on Brett's face when her name came up.

"When there's an unexpected death, as in the case of Miss Forbes, we tend to run a mini investigation while we wait for the coroner's report. We ran your name through the system and got a hit on a lady called Lily Banks. She made an assault allegation against you in January 2020."

Brett glared through his tears, "That charge was dropped, why are you digging around in my past as though I'm a suspect?"

Before Kevin could say anything more Piper leaned forward and passed him a business card out of her pocket.

"I'm a criminal lawyer DCI Greggs. I also represent Mr Folder, so please let me know if you wish to question him in an official capacity."

The underlying message was clear, this had been touted as a condolence call, and if it turned into anything else Kevin would be overstepping the mark.

"No Ms Daniels, there's nothing of an official nature to discuss."

Turning to Brett again Kevin thanked him for his time before leaving the house. Outside he got in his car and pulled away, something was still gnawing at his guts. The whole thing was off and he didn't like it. Kevin wasn't a man who believed in coincidences and two girlfriends dying in tragic accidents exactly a year apart didn't sit well with him.

He sighed, there was no point beating the drum about it. Both deaths had been ruled accidental, and unless any evidence came up to the contrary he'd had to add this one to the closed pile.

Chapter Three

FEBRUARY 2022 - STELLA CAULDWELL

Stella Cauldwell turned up her music and smiled to herself. This was their song, the one that'd been playing when they'd met. It felt like fate considering she was on her way to Brett's house for their first Valentine's Day.

Rewinding a few months, Stella thought about how New Year's Eve had felt as though it was going to be the worst night of her life. She'd broken up with her boyfriend just before Christmas and spent the festive season bawling her eyes out. Stella's best friend was determined she wouldn't be spending New Year listening to sad songs and feeling sorry for herself. She'd let herself into Stella's flat and tutted at the mess. Stella looked around at the debris of half-eaten selection boxes and glasses with the remnants of baileys cluttering up her coffee table. Her friend started to tidy up as she told Stella how they were going to spend New Year's Eve.

"Come on Stella, it's just the local pub. Give it a go, and if you're really unhappy we'll leave and toast New Year here with Big Ben."

How could she argue with that? Not that it meant she was going to put too much effort in when it came to getting ready. Throwing on some jeans, a blouse, and a light touch of make-up she'd almost changed her mind when Sue showed up and hustled her out of the house. The party was more fun than she'd thought it would be, but she still felt like the odd one out. No one else seemed to have the sheen of misery that she felt and eventually, Stella crept away to a dark corner with her drink. Sue was the life and soul of the party and despite her friend's earlier offer, she was reluctant to pull her away when she was clearly having that much fun.

When the man had first approached she'd been on guard, ready for him to try and hit on her she planned how to rebuff him. Polite but firm, she thought, no need to cause offence.

It hadn't worked out like that though, Brett was amusing and witty, and Stella found herself enjoying his company. He was friendly without being too much which made her feel safe. At midnight, after a few more drinks than she'd originally planned, she found herself kissing him. They'd exchanged numbers and she'd floated home with Sue congratulating herself on how she'd helped her friend move on from that cheating bastard who'd broken her heart.

His message the next day had made Stella smile, and still feeling bold from the drinks the night before she'd answered him with a mildly saucy reply. One thing led to another and she'd continued to find him witty and amusing. Their feelings had grown quickly and she wasn't ashamed to admit that she'd fallen in love. Stella knew he felt the same way, he'd told her so enough times. That was the other thing about him, he wasn't embarrassed to say I love you like a lot of men. Dating someone as emotionally mature as Brett made her realise how immature her exs had been.

The road was slippery with black ice, there'd been a freeze overnight and the driving conditions were treacherous. Local news was full of advice not to travel unless the journey was essential, but Stella believed this journey was essential, she couldn't imagine not seeing Brett tonight.

Hitting the sharp bends of a rural lane Stella tapped her brakes to slow down but nothing happened. If anything the car sped up and she felt the tyres slide across the icy surface.

"Shit"

She hissed the word out loud as she realised she'd have to pull over as soon as she could and ring Brett to come and get her. She couldn't risk driving a car without fully functioning brakes in this weather. Spotting a layby she twisted the wheel towards it and pressed harder on the brakes. They were spongy underfoot so she slammed her foot right down to the floor. Unfortunately, she hadn't corrected the steering so when the car failed to stop she found herself traveling at speed towards the layby. Trying desperately to correct it without slowing down caused the car to spin and skid. Stella hit the wooden fencing behind the layby splintering the wood and plunging through the gap she'd created. On the other side was a sheer drop. The car hung between safety and certain death for a few seconds, teetering on the edge of the embankment as though Stella might have a chance to survive.

It was a cruel false hope, Stella realised as the car tilted forward and dropped over the edge. The journey to the bottom was mercifully fast, Stella was barely aware of flipping over and over until the car exploded as it hit the ground.

DCI Greggs tore the dry crusts off his bacon sandwich and stacked them neatly on the side of his plate. It'd been another Valentine's Day without his partner and Kevin was feeling the usual mixture of bitterness and sorrow. Holidays and special occasions were the hardest for him, her birthday, their anniversary, and of course Christmas, New Year, and Valentine's Day. His parents were constantly trying to convince him it was time to get out there and meet someone else.

"Rachel wouldn't want you to be alone forever. Get out there Kev, open yourself up to the idea of moving on."

He'd nodded as though he agreed with them, but there was no chance he could even consider it while he still grieved Rachel so deeply. She'd been the other half of him, his soul mate. Kevin was a great believer that you only had one true love, and since he'd found and lost his, there was no one else out there for him.

"Nasty accident yesterday. I don't know what was worse, seeing what was left of that car or telling the poor bloke sitting at home waiting for her that his girlfriend was dead."

Kevin looked up as he caught the tail-end of the conversation, tuning in, he felt a spark of interest as he heard the rest.

"I couldn't believe it when I heard he lost another girlfriend last year to a tragic accident. Some people just seem to have nothing but shitty luck."

Pushing aside the remains of his breakfast Kevin cleared his throat to get the attention of the two traffic officers standing by his table.

"What was the boyfriend's name?"

They looked over, and realising he was a higher-ranking officer, immediately answered.

"Brett Folder sir. We found him at his house waiting for Stella to show up, he was completely devastated."

I'll bet, thought Kevin, dating Brett was apparently a dangerous game for his girlfriends.

"Anything suspicious about the accident?"

They shook their heads, and PC Williams answered, "No sir, not that we'd be able to tell considering the car blew up on impact. The roads are so icy it's almost impossible to find any evidence from before she left the road. The best we can piece together is that she was trying to pull into the layby when she lost control of the car. It hit the fencing at such a speed that it went right through and over the edge."

Despite the logic of their scenario, Kevin couldn't help but get that gut feeling again. He wasn't a fan of coincidences and this was way beyond that.

Kevin didn't really have the time to play Lone Ranger and poke around in a case that didn't officially exist. He couldn't leave it though. If Brett Folder had anything to do with these deaths he wanted to know. The only loose end he'd found so far was Lily Banks. Her mysterious disappearance didn't sit well with him, and now he was determined to find her. The last record he'd come across suggested she worked in a local pub in 2019. The Hare and Horse on the high street was a busy, popular place that often held live music events.

The landlord, Mike Evans, invited Kevin into the main bar when he'd flashed his warrant card at the front door. He'd looked irritated, and the reason became clear when Mike let out a stream of complaints before Kevin could explain what he was there for.

"It's harassment, that's what it is. This pub has been here for over a hundred years but when people move in nearby they do nothing but complain about us. What did they think was going to happen when they brought their house right by a pub that holds regular music events? It's like those idiots who move in by a church and then whinge about the bells sounding every Sunday. I'm sick of it, if they keep it up I'm worried it'll affect my licence."

Kevin quickly reassured him, "I'm not here about noise complaints sir. I don't work for the licencing team, I'm here about an ex-employee."

Mike looked relieved, "We had a band on a couple of nights ago for Valentine's night and I thought the neighbours had already lodged a load of new complaints. Which member of staff? We usually have a regular team here, I treat them well and they stay long-term."

"Lily Banks. I've got a record of her working here in 2019."

The landlord wrinkled his nose, "Ah yes her. I did wonder if that was who you meant. Lily only worked here for a few months before I had to let her go. She was alright at first, a bit quiet and serious, but she was reliable and worked hard. It wasn't until New Year's Eve that I found out she wasn't what I'd first thought. An ex-boyfriend came in with his new girlfriend and as soon as she spotted them she kicked off. Marched over there and started yelling at them both. Then she picked up a drink and poured it over the woman's head. I couldn't ignore that so I sent her straight home and told her not to bother coming back."

Interesting, thought Kevin, "Do you know who the ex-boyfriend was?"

Mike nodded, "He's pretty much a regular of ours. Brett Folder lives up the road from the pub so we're sort of his local."

Even more interesting, Kevin thought as he thanked Mike for his time and left. One of the last times he could find Lily around she'd had a row with Brett. Had he been so pissed off by her behaviour that he'd tracked her down later? If he had then maybe they'd had another fight. One that had ended with either Lily feeling the need to disappear, or even worse he'd killed her and hidden her body.

The assault allegation had been soon after the pub incident, a couple of days later in fact. Had Brett followed that up by killing her?

If Kevin was right, then Brett Folder could be a serial killer. A man who'd got away with killing for at least three years now. The problem was there wasn't anything that would justify opening this as a case.

Did he risk going back to Brett's house, or would his lawyer friend show up and get in the way like she had last time he'd tried? What he needed was to find someone who'd known Lily, someone who could give him some background on her relationship with Brett.

It had taken a lot of research, but Kevin had finally turned up a young woman who'd known Lily at college. They'd have known each other back when Lily first met Brett so it might pay some dividends.

Zita Bloom wrapped a curl around her finger as she listened to Kevin's reasons for needing to speak to her.

"I didn't know her that well, we were in a few of the same classes and sometimes she came along for drinks when we all went out. That was how she met that Brett bloke. We were all at the pub in a big group that he was part of and she got chatting to him, they exchanged numbers and started seeing each other after that."

Kevin nodded, "And how was the relationship between them?"

Zita shrugged, "I dunno really. She was excited when they exchanged numbers but she sort of dropped me after that. I think she got so involved with him there wasn't much space for anyone else. Not that I was bothered, like I said, I wasn't that close to her anyway. She could be a bit intense if you know what I mean."

The young woman paused as though thinking how best to explain it, "She tended to get really over-focused on stuff. Sometimes it was things like a project we'd been set. She'd do way above and beyond, and not because she wanted to impress anyone either, it was more that she couldn't help herself. Lily was the same with relationships too. If a bloke gave her his number she'd immediately be looking through wedding magazines."

Zita waved a hand in the air and Kevin noticed that she'd bitten her nails to the quick.

"I'm exaggerating, but she was prone to reading too much into things. One of the men she dated in our group said she'd message him constantly and just show up at his door all the time. Nothing too weird, just, well, intense."

"Did you know she made an allegation of assault against Brett?"

The woman gave a dismissive sniff, "By then we'd all graduated from college and started work and I hadn't seen her for ages. I heard about it, but I didn't make contact with her."

"When was the last time you saw her?"

That question made Zita think hard, "I'd have to say around the Summer of 2019, early Summer probably."

"Do you know much about her history from before you met her?"

Zita waggled her hand from side to side, "Lily wasn't big on talking about her past. She did tell me that both her parents were dead and that she grew up in care, but that was about all the detail I got."

Kevin thanked her for her time before leaving. He wasn't sure that anything he'd learned today was helpful, especially as he didn't officially have a case.

A butt-kicking always hurts however you looked at it, thought Kevin. When his boss had called him into his office it hadn't occured to him that he was in the shit. Kevin tended to keep his head down and not rattle the brass so bollockings were a rare occurrence.

"I've had a complaint, Greggs. Tell me why you've got a bug up your arse about Brett Folder? According to his lawyer, you've been poking around in his personal life without any good reason. Is that right?"

Kevin ducked his head to hide his annoyance, bloody Piper Daniels. Straightening his face he gave his boss a nod.

"I think three unexplained deaths around one man makes him of interest to the police, especially if there's also a potential missing person's case included."

His boss eyed him thoughtfully, "Piper Daniels is like a terrier with a rat when she gets her teeth into something. But then I also have to concede that being as she's close friends with Brett Folder it suggests that her interest isn't entirely professional."

Kevin knew this was a good time to keep quiet, if he didn't want to be closed down he was best letting his boss come to the right decision on his own.

"This isn't official business Greggs. You can poke about on the sidelines, but until you get some real evidence I don't want to hear about it from anyone. All of those cases were ruled as accidental deaths, and there's no official missing person's case that I'm aware of. Keep your head down and your nose clean – is that clear?"

That was probably the best he was going to get he thought as he gave his agreement and left the office. At least he hadn't been entirely shut out of the case, but he would need to find something more concrete than a gut feeling if he wanted to make it official.

Chapter Four

FEBRUARY 2023 - LUCY SHAW

This was quite possibly the best Valentine's that Lucy had ever had.

Lucy Shaw's love life hadn't been especially good in the last few years. The men she'd dated had either been less interested in getting serious than her, or they'd been cheating bastards who'd broken her heart. Then she'd met Brett Folder at a music gig and it'd been like everything had fallen into place as she'd looked into his eyes. Neither of them had wanted to waste any time so they'd become inseparable very quickly. When he'd told her about the past tragedies he'd endured her heart had gone out to him. It explained why he didn't want to risk having their first Valentine's Day in the UK, so here they were, sunning themselves in Tenerife. Instead of cold, wet, miserable weather, Lucy was waking up every day to blue skies and sunshine. The hotel had an amazing swim-up pool bar and that's where they'd been spending most of their time since arriving a couple of days ago.

Today was no exception, she'd left Brett heading up to the bar while she nipped back to their room to grab the book she'd left behind. Not that she expected to get much time to read it, Brett was so attentive that she didn't have an opportunity to read. Lucy dropped the book onto her sunbed, shed her sarong, and smiled at the member of staff who'd just walked by.

"Buenos dias, Senora."

Using one of her few words of Spanish she replied, "Hola" before giving him a friendly smile. It was a beautiful island, full of sunshine, smiles, and stunning sunsets. She'd never been here before but Brett had. He'd booked them into a lovely resort in a small town called Playa Arena. They were right near the black sand beach, and Lucy had got used to waking up to the sound of the waves crashing against the rocks. She hadn't known what to expect when they'd first arrived, but as soon as she saw the magnificent sight of the Los Gigantes cliffs looming over them she knew it was going to be fantastic. Even though they were all-inclusive Brett was a man after her own heart who wanted to explore the local area. He'd taken her for dinner at Panchos, a beachside restaurant, where they'd sat under a drooping palm tree and stared at the sea while they'd eaten fresh fish served with local Canarian potatoes. It was almost like a dream that Lucy hoped she never had to wake up from.

Lucy walked down the steps into the pool and dipped her warm shoulders into the cool water before pushing off to swim towards the railings. Lying on her back she floated by the edge looking up at the deep blue sky and the long leaves of the palm trees. This was bliss and she couldn't believe her luck.

When she felt something tangle in her hair from behind she didn't realise what was happening at first. It was a hand, fingers digging into her scalp as whoever it was clutched a handful of her hair. Lucy wriggled but all that succeeded in doing was to cause her head to go under the surface. Her open mouth filled with chlorinated pool water and she came back up coughing and spluttering. With barely a moment to draw breath so she could call out the hand drove her head into the hard concrete wall. The blow sent a spark of pain to her brain before mercifully, everything went dark.

The call from the British embassy took Kevin by surprise, especially when he found out what they calling about. It appeared that a British national had drowned whilst on holiday in Tenerife and her partner, Brett Folder, would need support from the local police force when he returned to the UK. The woman from the embassy was light on details, all she knew was that Lucy Shaw appeared to have drowned in a busy swimming pool at their hotel. She passed on a number to contact the Guardia Civil officer in charge of the case and said a hasty goodbye.

Kevin didn't hesitate to dial the number, another accidental death of one of Brett's girlfriends, but this time in another country. Was he getting smarter and committing his murders overseas?

The Guardia Civil officer was polite, but not especially helpful with details. His name was Juan Melian, and although his English was heavily accented it was almost fluent.

"I am sorry for my poor English."

Kevin laughed and gave the typically British response, "Better than my Spanish!"

"Lucy Shaw was here on holiday with her novio, sorry, boyfriend, Brett Folder. He was at the bar and

Lucy had gone to her room for her book. She came down and said hello to a member of staff before getting in the pool. One of the guests alerted the socarrista, uh lifeguard. He pulled her out but it was too late. It looks as though she banged her head on the side of the pool hard enough to knock herself out."

"Are there any suspicious circumstances?"

The voice on the other end of the line replied quickly, "No, this is just a tragic accident. Sadly this happens a lot here on the island. The tourists they drink a little too much and aren't as careful as they would be at home."

After hanging up Kevin couldn't stop thinking about it. Brett Folder with yet another alibi when the unthinkable happens to yet another of his girlfriends. Going out with Brett must be like getting the kiss of death, he thought.

That gave Kevin another idea, could he prove that Brett's alibis weren't as ironclad as everyone thought they were? Pulling out the files he also considered a second possibility, was Brett getting someone to do the dirty work for him? He threw that idea in the bin where it belonged, why would he? If he was doing this it was because he enjoyed it and he'd be doing it to get his thrills up close and personal.

Making a note of the accident time and Brett's location when he was informed, Kevin picked up his keys and set off to the first accident location. The tube station wasn't as busy as it would've been when Ruby had slipped in front of a train, but for the purposes of his experiment that didn't matter.

Kevin jogged down the platform and mentally performed the act of shoving someone. Would Brett have waited a moment and watched as Ruby plummeted off the edge? Did he wait enough time to make sure she was dead or did he turn around and head straight off?

Kevin decided Brett was far too cautious to wait around, spinning on his heel he jogged out of the station and ran to the next one on the same line. He wheezed a little as he hopped onto the train and leaned against the pole to catch his breath. At the stop nearest to the restaurant he fast walked to the closed door and checked the timer he'd set on his phone.

Just enough time, he thought. If Brett was quick and efficient he'd have had no trouble pushing Ruby under a train and making it here in time to be sat at a table waiting for the police to come and break the news.

Next was Mandy Forbes. That was a simple one. She'd been just up the road from their house when she'd fallen in front of a lorry. Brett would've had ample time to get from the house to where she was waiting to cross the road, give her a shove, and then go back home. Looking up and down the street, he wondered about a man who could coldly kill a woman before going home and patiently waiting for the police to arrive.

Kevin headed back to the office, Stella's accident was the easiest of them all. Brett would simply have had to tamper with her car while she was at work so that once she got behind the wheel it was all ready for her fatal accident. Lucy's was more difficult. To work that one out he'd need to go to Tenerife, but he was pretty sure his boss wouldn't give him the time of day to open an international case based on what he had. If the UK police were going to get involved outside of the country it took a lot of mediation and discussion first.

That's not to say he couldn't do it in his own time though. A bit of sunshine wouldn't go amiss, all he had to do was book some holiday and get a flight over there.

His boss had given him a long hard look when he'd approached asking for some last minute annual leave.

"Where are you thinking of going DCI Greggs?"

"I thought I'd get a bit of sunshine, maybe one of the Canary Islands."

His boss had shaken his head, "I'm going to take a punt that you're planning to pop up in Tenerife poking around in the accident they called about. You need to stop it and back off DCI Greggs. There's no evidence this wasn't just another tragic accident, and if it wasn't we have to trust that the Spanish police will deal with it. It's not our business, and if you go over there stirring things up you'll create a stink that I'll have to deal with."

Kevin smiled as he placed his bags in the plastic trays that would slide through the scanners. He'd semi-convinced his boss that this was nothing more than a short break away. Kevin had also promised not to cause an international incident, so he was sure his boss was aware that he wouldn't be able to help himself when it came to having a nosy around. Kevin had managed to get a room at the same hotel Brett and Lucy had stayed at. Should be handy to see the place it happened, and it might help him get a mental picture of the scene.

He wasn't a big fan of flying and he tended to stick to places that were only a couple of hours away from the UK usually. The last time Kevin had been to Tenerife it was to Las Americas with a few mates in his twenties. He remembered the heat and the cheap alcohol, and his best friend throwing up on the patch, but according to what he'd read this part wasn't like that. He hoped not, he was definitely too old now for the party all-night clubbing district.

The flight was everything Kevin hated. A small child spent almost all of the just over four-hour journey kicking the back of his chair, and a few rows back a hen party screeched and whooped the entire time they were in the air. A nearby group of tourists who were old enough to know better were passing a bottle of duty-free vodka around and becoming increasingly difficult to manage for the staff. One in particular seemed to feel it was appropriate to make lewd comments to the female stewardess. By the halfway mark, Kevin decided he couldn't sit back and not do anything anymore. Getting out of his seat he made his way up to the group.

"I think that's enough now folks, I suggest you just settle down and save it for when you get there."

Kevin wasn't surprised that his advice was greeted by jibes and suggestions that he fuck off and mind his own business. At this point, he pulled his trump card and flashed his police ID.

"We can always make this official if you'd prefer?"

The group fell silent and as Kevin returned to his seat the stewardess appeared with a can of lager and a wide smile.

"On the house, officer, thank you for intervening."

When they finally landed and disembarked Kevin was hit by the heat like a physical punch. He'd dressed for the weather he'd left behind and before he'd even cleared passport control the sweat was rolling down his back and making his skin clammy. The package deal included transport, so Kevin made his way across the road to the designated bus stop where he climbed aboard the coach. He enjoyed the journey to the hotel. The scenery was amazing, palm trees, cliffs, and small clusters of houses and apartments kept him staring out of the window the whole time. When the coach pulled up outside his hotel he wheeled his case in and collected his room key.

Kevin took a quick shower and changed into clothes more suited to the weather before wandering down to the pool area. No time like the present to start asking a few questions, he thought.

The smiling woman at the pool bar spoke fairly good English. When she caught sight of his warrant card she quickly filled him in on what she knew.

"I was working that day, I remember the man coming to the bar and how upset he was when he found out his novia was dead."

Kevin frowned, "Novia?"

"Ahh, sorry, yes I think you say girlfriend?"

Thanking her, and taking note of the new word to add to his limited supply of Spanish, he asked about the timing.

"Was Mr Folder at the bar the whole time?"

She nodded, and then shrugged, "I was busy, I thought so, but maybe he went to the bathroom or moved away. I didn't see him all the time that he was waiting for the lady."

Kevin added this information to the rest of his timelines. Looking at the pool and where Lucy was found floating there was plenty of time for Brett to get to her, smack her head on the side, and get back to the bar as though he'd never left. It was yet another hole in Brett's story and his suspicions of the man were deepening.

Deciding to try the local beer, Dorada, Kevin wandered over to an empty table where he got out his notebook and started writing down what he knew so far. When a shadow fell over him he assumed at first that it was one of the staff checking if he wanted another drink. Looking up he found himself eye to eye with a grim-faced Guardia Civil officer.

"Hola Senor. I am Juan Melian, I believe we spoke on the phone about Lucy Shaw?"

Juan placed two bottles of Dorada on the table and pulled up a chair, "I am going off duty, but my cousin called and let me know you were here and asking questions. What is it about this accident that brings an English policeman all the way to my island?"

Kevin took a swig out of the fresh beer and offered Juan a smile, "I'm not here officially, it's more of a personal interest."

The Guardia Civil officer cocked his head, "Tell me everything."

Considering Kevin didn't have much it was surprising how long it took to tell Juan about it. Enough time that they ordered another round of beers.

When he'd done, Juan looked interested, "I agree, the whole thing is very strange. Unfortunately, I can not do much to help you. Miss Shaw's death has been ruled an accident and we are no longer looking into the case. Mr Folder has left Spain and returned to the UK so there is nothing we can do anyway."

He went quiet for a moment, "That is the official line out of the way. Unofficially, I am like you. I do not like to let go of a case if I have what you call a "gut feeling." If there is anything I can do to help while you are here, you must call me, and if you ever get the answers you are looking for I would be interested in hearing the outcome."

It was the closest Kevin was going to get to permission to investigate in this man's patch. The problem was, he wasn't sure he was going to find anything concrete either.

The cold grey skies of the UK looked twice as depressing after Kevin's time in the sunshine. He'd enjoyed his impromptu trip even though he hadn't come up with anything helpful apart from the theory that Brett could've killed her. No one had seen him leave the bar and his reaction to her death had appeared genuine to everyone who'd witnessed it. Despite that, Kevin couldn't shake the feeling that Brett was involved somehow.

Last year he'd met a forensic psychiatrist on a case, and Kevin thought back to what he'd said about how psychopaths learned to mimic emotions. Was Brett a clever psychopath who knew exactly how to behave to throw everyone off the scent?

It was as though the car had a mind of its own as it pulled up outside Brett's house. No harm in checking how Brett was, Kevin thought. After all, that's what the consulate worker had suggested when they'd called him.

Brett didn't appear to be glad to see him when he answered the door. Glaring down from the doorstep he demanded to know what Kevin wanted.

"Surely with the crime rate in this country, you've got far more important things to be getting on with than bugging me?"

Kevin shrugged and smiled in what he hoped was a friendly way, "We're never too busy to check on a local citizen who suffered a tragic loss abroad."

Brett didn't look convinced, but he was about to let Kevin into his house when Piper appeared behind him.

"DCI Greggs, and what can we do for you? It seems the only time we ever see you is when you've come to rub salt into my friend's wounds about a recent loss."

Ohhh spiteful, thought Kevin, if those words were real barbs he'd have more holes in him than a teabag.

"Just checking on Mr Folder's well-being considering the distressing accident that killed his girlfriend a week ago."

Piper huffed, "Nice tan you've got there DCI Greggs. Been on holiday? I don't suppose if I checked I'd find you've been to Tenerife would I?"

Kevin didn't allow his irritation to show on his face, "I'm sure where I take my holidays isn't of interest to anyone Ms Daniels."

Turning to Brett he held out his hand for a shake, "My condolences sir. You've got my card, please let me know if there's anything I can do."

Brett reluctantly shook his hand before mumbling a thank you and shutting the door in Kevin's face. DCI Greggs stood on the path for a moment, both Brett and Piper came across as being defensive and reluctant to talk to him. If Brett had nothing to hide why would he avoid engaging with the police?

Chapter Five

FEBRUARY 14TH 2024 - CARA EDWARDS

Cara Edwards wondered why she'd ever thought it was a good idea to buy Brett's Valentine's gift in person rather than ordering it online like all the sensible people did.

An elderly woman had just run over her foot with a pull-along shopping bag, a small child was screaming right next to her, and a group of young people were pushing and shoving each other nearby. Cara hated the high street. She usually avoided it, but in a moment of sentimentality, she'd decided it would be more personal to come out and choose Brett's gift. She didn't often let her emotions make the decisions, but there was something about Brett that made her act out of character.

They'd met on this very high street. Brett was just coming out of a shop with his arms full of bags when she almost ran into him. She was carrying a cup of take-out coffee that she'd dropped when she came up short to avoid the collision and Brett had quickly offered to buy her a replacement. They'd chosen to drink it in the cafe where it was warm and cosy. The steamed up front window protected them from the outside world and the smells of fried food and toast made her stomach rumble. Brett had turned out to be so entertaining and charming that she'd lost track of time and before leaving they'd arranged another date. Fast forward four months and here she was trying to find him the perfect gift.

Cara had also purchased a new, sexy outfit to wear that night. She had no idea where he was taking her which added to the excitement, she'd tried to trick him into telling her by sending a photo of the dress and asking if it was suitable. Brett had replied with googly eyes and enigmatically replied "Very suitable." Brett was deliciously impulsive, and Cara was enjoying every moment of it. The bag that contained a bottle of mid-range champagne was biting into her hand so she shifted it to the other one while she leaned forward to look into the window of the shop in front of her.

Would he like the elegant port, cheese, and glasses set, she mused to herself. It looked like something he'd enjoy, but indecision held her at the window wondering if she should keep looking for something else. Cara had just made her mind up to go in and get it when she felt a sharp punch to her side. It knocked the wind out of her and she gasped for breath.

Putting her hand to the spot where she'd been hit she felt a warm, sticky substance. Looking down Cara realised she hadn't been punched, she'd been stabbed. Blood soaked through her heavy coat and ran down her leg, suddenly light-headed she leaned against the window. A second stabbing pain in her other side brought her to her knees. The crowd had noticed by this time and she was surrounded by people. The last thing Cara heard was a voice demanding an ambulance.

Kevin heard the shout on his police radio in his car. Screeching to a halt he quickly reversed and headed in the direction of the high street. He'd usually leave this sort of call to the uniforms but he'd been waiting for an incident like this. Although it wasn't an accident like the others Kevin wanted to check and make sure it wasn't linked to Brett Folder.

The woman was covered by a blanket, that, and the ambulance not being in any hurry, suggested the victim was beyond help. The forensic team was on its way, but in the meanwhile one of the uniforms had got the woman's mobile out of her bag and was busy scrolling through it to find her next of kin.

Kevin approached him and peered over his shoulder, "Anything interesting?"

The uniform jumped at the sound of a senior officer right behind him, "Only this text sir. She appears to have sent a photo of a dress to a man called Brett Folder. I think he must be her partner, shall I look for an address on the system?"

Kevin shook his head, "No need, I know exactly where to find Mr Folder."

This was it, he thought, this time it was obviously not an accident. Had Brett dropped himself in it by stabbing this one? As it was actually a murder he now had a good enough reason to bring Brett in.

"I need you and your partner to get over there and break the news, I'll follow on in my car and potentially we're going to need to take him in for questioning."

Arriving at Brett's house, Kevin was disappointed when he didn't get a reply to his knock on the door.

"We need to put out an alert on Mr Folder's car, he needs to be picked up as soon as he's seen and brought to the station."

The two uniforms looked a little puzzled by his eagerness to get to Brett, but they wouldn't question a senior officer. Kevin turned to walk back to his car. He was impatient to get his chance to question Mr Folder as he had a feeling that this time he'd be able to prove what his gut was telling him. As he gave one last look around, he spotted a familiar figure approaching from up the road.

It was Brett Folder, and inevitably he had Piper Daniels behind him. Kevin immediately stopped still and blocked his entry to his front door.

Brett scowled at him, "Not you again. What is it this time?"

"Do you know a woman called Cara Edwards?"

Folder's scowl dropped, "Yes. God don't tell me something's happened to her too?"

Kevin narrowed his eyes at what he saw as Brett's play-acting, "Mr Folder I am arresting you on suspicion of murder. You do not have to say anything, but it may harm your defence if you do not mention anything that you later rely on in court. Anything you do say may be used as evidence against you. Do you understand the caution?"

Brett stepped backward and almost fell onto PC Long. Kevin watched as the cuffs were snapped onto his wrists and Brett was led over to the uniform's car. The man stumbled and protested all the way there, and Kevin couldn't help but be impressed by how convincing he was.

Piper shoved Kevin out of the way so she could call over to Brett, "Don't say a word until I get there Brett. Keep it zipped and we'll work out our strategy when I've got the full facts in front of me."

As the car pulled away she glared at Kevin, "Nice work officer, finally got what you wanted did you? I've got no idea why you want to pin this on my friend, but you won't get away with it."

There wasn't a lot Kevin could say to that. It was untrue of course, he wasn't going around fitting up innocent people, but there were questions to be answered.

Pushing the sausage roll around his plate Kevin took an unwanted swig of his water. He hadn't actually been at all hungry, he'd just wanted to goad Brett and his stuck-up brief when he'd announced the snack break. It was a good tactic to leave the prisoner to sweat for a bit, especially after dumping those photos "accidentally" in front of him. Brett's reaction had been very interesting, he mused to himself, the way he'd reared back from them. He'd heard it said that a killer didn't like to look at his victims, maybe that was the case with Folder.

A loud ding alerted him that an email had just arrived on his phone, opening it he scowled at the screen. Bloody CPS reckoned he didn't have enough to charge Folder and if he didn't get a confession or any real evidence in the next two hours he'd have to bail him.

Shit, fuck, and bollocks. What a wanky mess this was, if he hadn't managed to get anything concrete in the last five years how the absolute fuck was he going to get something in two hours?

Pushing aside his plate of half-eaten sausage roll he stood up, if he was on the clock there was no time to waste pissing about pretending to eat.

Marching back into the room a few minutes later Kevin carefully set his face into the same self-satisfied look that he'd left with. There was no point letting them pick up on his disappointment because if they did it was game over. Piper Daniels was drumming her fingers on the table impatiently. She shot Kevin the bog eye as he came back into the room.

"I don't have all day DCI Greggs, either you plan to charge my client or you'll be releasing him, which is it?"

Kevin shot her a smirk as though he was holding back something vital, "I've got a few more questions, and I'd suggest your client should consider answering them. This is his opportunity to tell his side of the story."

He was rewarded by a flicker of anxiety crossing Brett's face, sitting down Kevin started the tape and introduced everyone in the room.

"Firstly Mr Folder, I'd like to ask about your alibi when Cara Edwards was being stabbed. The other victims may have been ruled accidental deaths, but Cara is a murder investigation."

Brett chewed his lip nervously, "I was shopping for Cara's Valentine's gift."

Kevin cocked his head to one side, "Where were you shopping Mr Folder? It wasn't on the high street was it?"

The answer was clear in Brett's expression of anxiety, "Yes, but I didn't see Cara. I swear I didn't see or do anything to her. Why would I? I loved her."

Piper winced and Kevin was sure she was going to be speaking to Brett later about making sudden proclamations to the police while under caution.

"I'd also like to talk to you about Lily Banks. I believe she was an ex-girlfriend of yours. One who we haven't been able to track down to speak to."

This time the look on Brett's face was more annoyance than anxiety, "What do you need to know about her for? The woman's mad as a box of frogs and twice as crazy."

Kevin shrugged, "Her name came up in our inquiries. She lodged an allegation of assault against you which she then dropped before vanishing. We'd like to hear her account of that, but unfortunately, we don't seem to be able to find her."

Brett ducked his head so Kevin couldn't see his expression, "I've got no idea where she is, in fact, I'm bloody glad she's gone. If I never see her again it'll be too soon."

"That's a lot of anger Mr Folder. From what I've heard you were very angry when she kicked off at your new girlfriend. Did you find her later Mr Folder, maybe pay her back?"

This time Brett's face flushed bright red and he slammed his fist on the table, "That's enough! The woman is a headcase. A stalker. One of those fatal attraction nutters."

Kevin leaned back in his chair, "Why don't you tell me about her?"

Chapter Six

FEBRUARY 2024 - BRETT FOLDER & LILY BANKS

I met Lily on a night out with friends. We'd gone to some dive out of town and she was sort of on the peripherals of the group. I got chatting with her and we exchanged numbers before going home. I should've worked out what she was like when I got up the next day to find a text already waiting for me in my inbox. It was just a casual one about how nice it'd been to meet me so I didn't think much of it. I didn't even bother replying that day. That night I got another one asking if I was blanking her. I replied and said of course not, I was just hungover and getting an early night.

When she suggested we meet for a drink I decided I may as well see where things led. We met at a local pub and while it was okay there wasn't a big spark between us. She seemed keen on me though, and we drifted along meeting up occasionally for drinks or a meal. I was at a loose end and thought it was a casual relationship with no strings, but Lily seemed to see it differently.

It was little things to start with, like the way she overreacted if I didn't reply to her messages soon enough or didn't answer her calls. I tried a few times to have a conversation with her about us and I was always honest that this wasn't a serious relationship for me. Lily would agree and then she'd fall back into the same behaviours. By Christmas 2018 I was starting to find it all a bit too much. I'd look out of my window and see her standing across the road staring at the house. I must admit I was too much of a coward to approach her so I just ignored it and hoped she'd stop of her own accord.

Christmas was a turning point for me, Lily was obsessed with it and suggested I come to her family's house with her. That was the final nail in our coffin. There was no way I wanted to spend the whole festive season with her family and I certainly didn't want to encourage her either. It was time to stop giving her false hope and to be upfront. I chickened out of doing it over the holidays, but I did refuse to go to her parents for Christmas Day which I hoped was a big hint. Instead, I went to Piper's house as I always did.

I've known her and her family since we were children so it was a tradition that I always spent at least one of the holidays there.

We'd eaten our meal and were all sat around watching tele and letting our food go down when suddenly Piper pointed out of the window. She ran over and announced that Lily was outside.

"She must've followed us here," Piper reckoned, but when I went to look she'd gone. It freaked me out though and from that day on I was always looking over my shoulder to make sure she wasn't behind me. I jumped at the imagined sound of footsteps every time I went out and I peered around the curtains to check she wasn't standing across the road. I got so paranoid I believed she was always there and nothing anyone could say would convince me otherwise.

Although Lily wasn't happy about my avoidance of a family Christmas, she still didn't seem to get the idea that it was over. She could be incredibly single-minded with a refusal to consider anything that didn't agree with her viewpoint. I let it drag on because I didn't want to trigger anything over New Year, but once that was over I sat her down and told her the bad news. She shrugged and said fine and I was hopeful that maybe she'd met someone else. It turned out that the only reason she hadn't been bothered was because she was planning to ignore what I'd said. It really didn't seem to have sunk in that I meant it, or maybe she was just so obsessed it was impossible for her to hear me.

After that, it was ten times worse. Lily showed up on my doorstep at all hours, following me to work, and hanging around my house. Piper told me I should take out an injunction against her, but it just seemed more hassle than it was worth. As we got into February she started sending me texts about Valentine's Day and I knew I had to put a stop to it. The next time I saw her outside my house I went over to her. She tried to hug me, but I pushed her away and told her in no uncertain terms that if I saw her near the house again I'd be calling the police. I was rude, blunt, and hurtful. I needed her to get the message this time, but it didn't feel good to treat anyone like that.

The problem was it seemed to just roll off her back. If she didn't want to hear it she closed her ears and blocked it out. Her hanging around my house and stalking me didn't change. She was more careful, but I knew she was out there. I was still getting messages from her and on Valentine's Day she posted an engagement ring and card through my letterbox. The card was "To my fiancee." and from then on she wrote me messages about our "engagement."

It was completely out there, she was asking what I thought of venues for our engagement party, and who I'd like to invite. I started to dread hearing the ding of a text and I refused to open them. Piper thought I should block her, but I was worried she'd find out and it'd make her worse. I guess I was hoping that if I ignored her she'd eventually get bored and move on.

In the meanwhile, I'd met Ruby at a gig at a local pub. She was funny and witty, and there were the sparks that'd been missing with Lily. We started seeing each other and by Christmas, we were pretty serious. We decided to go to the pub we'd met at for New Year's Eve only to find that Lily was working there. I was sure it was intentional that she got a job there, but how would I prove it? I'd already told Ruby about her and she insisted that we stay when I suggested we just leave and find somewhere else to see in the New Year. I think Ruby hoped that because Lily was at work it might stop her saying anything, but I could've told her it'd be fruitless.

She started with glares and dirty looks, and then it was muttered comments as she walked by the table. You'd have thought I was cheating on her by the way she was behaving. Eventually, I told her to leave us alone to enjoy our night or I'd have to speak to her boss. Lily was furious, she picked up my half-drunk pint from the table and tipped the contents over Ruby's head.

"Take that you man-stealing slut."

I remember staring at her in horror, "What the fuck do you think you're playing at?"

By this time her boss noticed and came over. Seeing Lily with the empty glass and Ruby dripping beer it didn't long to work out what had happened. They sacked her on the spot and insisted on comping us drinks for the rest of the night to make up for it. Ruby was a good sport, even soaked in beer she insisted that we stay and make the most of the night.

I couldn't help but feel anxious though, it spoiled the night for me because I was constantly looking over my shoulder waiting for Lily to make another appearance. She didn't, and I couldn't see her when we left the pub either. All I could hope was that seeing me with someone else had finally drummed the message home. I was lucky, Ruby stood by me, and if anything it made us closer. Losing her on Valentine's Day was devastating and now you suspect me of doing something to her.

And not just her either, you seem to think I'm a prolific serial killer with a weird fetish for Valentine's Day.

Chapter Seven

Kevin had made careful notes all through Brett's story, "So, why didn't you come to the police about the stalking and harassment?"

Brett shrugged, "I was embarrassed I guess. A grown man complaining that a woman is frightening him. With hindsight, I should've done, maybe you could've put a stop to it."

"Do you think Lily is dangerous Mr Folder?"

There was a moment while Brett and Piper exchanged a look that suggested they were still holding something back.

"Come on, one of you needs to tell me exactly what's going on. Four dead women and another one missing is serious, and unless you tell me differently, it currently looks as though it's Mr Folder who is the consistent link in my case."

Piper gave Brett a small nod that encouraged him to speak, "I think she was just being over dramatic, but of course, with what's happening it takes on a more sinister meaning. Piper tried talking to her but it didn't go well and Piper ended up warning Lily that we'd take legal action against her if she didn't stop harassing me. Lily's response was to say "If I can't have him no one will."

Kevin turned his gaze to Piper, "Is that right Ms Daniels?"

She sighed, "When Brett refused to report her behaviour to the police I offered to try and speak to her. It wasn't long before an opportunity arose, she was hanging around outside Brett's house so I went out and asked her to come for a chat. She heard me out, but when I'd finished she just laughed at me. "You just don't understand us. We're engaged to be married whether you like it or not." That's when I understood nothing I said would make any difference, there was no getting through to her. I told her she was leaving us with no choice but to take out an injunction against her."

Piper paused before continuing, "That's when she stopped laughing and I saw the real risk she posed. "I wouldn't do that if I were you. If I can't have him, no one will." It was chilling how coldly she said it, and when I went back inside we looked out the window and there she was, back watching the house again."

"When was the last time either of you saw her?"

Brett had a think, "I'd say early January 2020."

Piper didn't need time to work it out, "For me it was before that. Probably December 2019. When Brett started getting serious with Ruby I didn't go over to his as often so I wasn't really around to see her hanging around outside his house like before."

There was one more thing that Kevin needed to know about, "And what's the real story behind the assault allegation Lily made against you on January 6th, 2020 Mr. Folder? Please don't lie to me, I need the whole truth right now."

Brett blushed, "I saw her outside the house and I lost my temper. It was less than a week since she'd poured a drink over Ruby and I'd had enough. I stormed out there and told her to fuck off and leave me alone. It didn't matter how blunt I was though Lily still didn't get it and I ended up grabbing her arm and shaking her. Luckily I managed to get control of myself before I did anything worse. Lily went straight to the police and told them I'd assaulted her, I was so ashamed, I've never laid a hand on a woman before. Piper offered to speak to her about dropping the charges, but I told her not to. If it looked as though I was trying to manipulate her it would look worse for me. It didn't matter anyway, because she dropped the charges a few days later."

Kevin's eyes darted from one to the other, "And neither of you coerced her into dropping the charges?"

Brett and Piper both shook their heads and then added a no out loud for the tape. There wasn't much else he could ask them right now, not without looking into this information first. It certainly hadn't provided him with anything tangible that would convince the CPS to allow a charge, which meant he'd have to release Brett on bail.

"I'm going to be releasing you on bail Mr Folder. You will have conditions to remain at your address, to report to the station weekly, and not to leave the country."

Kevin couldn't miss the smug look of triumph on Piper's face but he ignored it. She may have won this battle, he thought, but she was far from winning the war. If he got so much as a sniff that her friend had anything to do with those women's deaths he'd be dragging him back down here.

DS Harding came up trumps with his deep dive into Lily's past.

"A friend of my sister's works in social services and when I explained what I was looking for and why, she was very helpful. Lily's parents died in a house fire when she was thirteen and with no other living relatives she was placed in care. Her records show her moving from placement to placement but the social worker I spoke to wouldn't, or couldn't, elaborate on why. I've also managed to dig up the name and address of one of her foster families."

Kevin looked thoughtfully at the whiteboard he'd been adding to, "So, we've got a young woman with a challenging history. Both Brett and her friend described Lily as being intense and obsessional. That doesn't mean she's killed anyone on its own, but it does make her a credible suspect."

Harding picked things up, "Brett isn't exactly Mr Squeaky Clean either. The links between him and the victims is the strongest so far. Plus the women he was seeing were often those who didn't have close friends or family leaving him their main focus."

Playing devil's advocate, Kevin tapped Brett's photo on the board, "But we have no evidence that he's done anything to any of them. All of them are accidental deaths apart from the last one. Cara's stabbing is the only official murder case we've got to hang our hats on. Plus it's the only one he hasn't got an alibi for."

His colleague nodded, "Even if you find footage of him being in town at the time Cara was stabbed he's already explained that by telling us he was there to buy her a gift."

Kevin scowled, "He must think he's being really clever, If it was him, I wonder what his motivation was for straying from his usual strategy of making the deaths look like an accident?"

Harding shrugged, but that thought had given Kevin an idea. His boss probably wouldn't sanction it officially, but he was sure he could get an off-the-record opinion from someone who might know the answer to that question.

Dr Ethan Quinn had been happy to help unofficially. Kevin knew him through a case last year and thanks to Dr Quinn he'd ended up making sure a dangerous psychopath stayed behind bars. Rather than log Ethan as a visitor to the station Kevin and Harding met up with him at his home. They waited impatiently while he read the files making notes as he worked through them.

Finally, he pushed them away and sat back in his chair, "Both of your suspects have red flags that I find pertinent to the case. Let's start with Brett Folder as he's your main focus."

Ethan pulled his notes over and used them to prompt his profile.

"Outwardly Mr Folder presents as being a well-rounded individual who only has one previous link to the police which he's managed to neatly explain away. Look under the surface however, and you find a man who jumps from one relationship to another very quickly. He's barely mourned one loss before he's replaced her. Not only does he move on rapidly, but these relationships become serious within a month or two. The women seem to build everything around him and it looks as though they become isolated from their usual support networks or don't have one to start with. This is a red flag for coercive behaviour, and often this is perpetrated by those who seek to abuse their partners without outside interference. This is only my professional opinion, I'd be able to tell you more if I could have an opportunity to meet with Mr Folder one to one."

Kevin shook his head, "I'd love to put you in a room with him but I can't see my boss agreeing to it. Let alone what his best friend slash lawyer would say about that."

Ethan smiled, "Maybe Mr Folder would appreciate a psychiatric assessment to ensure that he's not being unduly stressed by your investigation? He's been through a lot of bereavement and as such it would stand to reason that he might be finding the additional pressure of being questioned as a suspect traumatic."

That made Kevin smile back, "Good point Doc. I'll keep that in mind. If it is Brett that's responsible, why would he veer away from his usual method of killing?"

"If Brett is our killer then he'll be fixed more on the date than the method. While it might be ideal to plan the murders to look like accidents, that won't be as hard and fast as the date. If he was left with no opportunity to hide his murder in an accident he'd have been pushed into going with whatever means met his objective. It looks as though the killer took a knife with them so I can only assume that was the case at all of the murders. Taking a weapon would then suggest they already had a plan B."

That made sense to Kevin, "And what about Lily Banks? What do you make of her history and her likelihood of being our murderer?"

The smile dropped from Ethan's face at the mention of Lily, "This is a young woman who rings a lot of alarm bells for me. She had a huge trauma in the form of losing both her parents and ending up in care. Throughout her formative years, she had no security as she moved from placement to placement. It's understandable that as an adult she became very contained and isolated. Trust is developed at a young age and she would've found it hard to open herself up to people. I'm also interested in the descriptions of her being "intense" and "obsessive." Those traits are the most concerning to me. She reads like someone who potentially wouldn't follow the social norms of building relationships with others. I see a lot of stalking type behaviours here, and we know that stalkers can become violent if confronted with reality."

Harding sighed, "So what next Doc? We need to get more of a handle on which of these two are the most likely suspects."

"I'd suggest a deep dive in their pasts. Often the answers will be found in the events that shaped them. Kevin said there's a foster family you can interview about Lily, is there anyone you can speak to about Brett's history?"

Kevin was thoughtful for a moment, "So far just Piper, and as she's his brief as well as his friend it'd be difficult to justify interviewing her and creating a conflict of interest."

Harding nudged his boss, "But does it have to be an interview boss? Couldn't we ask her as his friend to tell us why she doesn't think he should be our chief suspect?"

Clapping the DS on the shoulder Kevin grinned at him, "I think you've just found us the perfect way in!"

Turning to Dr Quinn, Kevin put his hands together as though begging, "I don't suppose you'd be willing to look at what we get as it comes in would you?"

Ethan chuckled, "You've got me interested now, I can hardly say no and then never find out if I was right."

Chapter Eight

Lily's foster carer had a warm smile and a mop of unruly curls that she kept pushing out of her face with an impatient hand. Kevin could see straight away that she'd be a welcome presence to a child who was probably frightened and confused when they arrived at her house. Misty Groves had a small child planted on her hip. The little boy looked a few months old and was winding and unwinding his grubby, sticky hand in her curls.

"Ouch Mikey, that hurt."

Misty gently untangled his plump little fist from her hair and waved the two officers into her house.

"Best we talk inside, that way, I can put this little monkey in his playpen before he yanks out all my hair and gives me a bald spot."

Mikey frowned when he was first lowered into his playpen, but as soon as he spotted the toys he gave a cheeky grin and crawled away to grab them. Misty had already made them a coffee along with a plate of biscuits. Scott didn't need much urging before he dipped his hand over the plate and grabbed up a chocolate digestive. Kevin bit back a smile, Scott's reputation as a snack hoover was well deserved.

"So, you want to talk about Lily Banks? I can't say I'm surprised, I always thought someone would come to me about her one day."

Kevin's ears pricked up, that sounded promising.

"Thank you Mrs Groves, any help you can give us will be greatly appreciated."

Misty waved her hand dismissively, "Please, call me Misty, Mrs Groves makes me feel really old! Lily was with me for less than a year, I'd say about seven months in total. It wasn't her shortest placement, but it was close to it. When she first arrived she was fourteen years old and already a veteran of the system. We were her third placement in a year and I could tell from her expression she wasn't expecting this one to last either. That just made me even more determined to make it work. Until Lily, I hadn't met a child that I couldn't get through to but she tested me to a point where I started to wonder if I was cut out for this job."

She sipped her coffee and Kevin could see how sad the memory made her look.

"We call the first month the honeymoon period. Nearly every child is on their best behaviour to start with, but Lily made it clear how she felt about us from day one. She barely spoke to us, and when she did it was with a tone that suggested it was under duress. Then she started playing cruel pranks on us all. She'd sneak into the bedrooms and take personal belongings, nothing big, mostly small items that she knew meant a lot to the owner. Then she'd leave them in another child's room to be found later. Of course, it would cause huge arguments and fights, and Lily would stand back and watch with this smug little smile as though enjoying the drama she'd caused. I was already at the end of my tether with her by the time she escalated and was removed from our home."

Misty looked uncomfortable, "I'm hoping I'm not overstepping by telling you, but I'm assuming this is something serious enough to warrant it. Lily became obsessed by one of her male teachers at school. She'd leave him little notes in his desk, and make excuses to hang around after class and walk him to his car. Other teachers and her social worker tried to address it with her, but she just shrugged them off. We were about a week away from a meeting to discuss how to manage it when she took things to the next level. Lily found out where the teacher lived and showed up at his house. He looked outside and there she was, standing across the road staring over. From then on she made it part of her daily routine, and no matter what we tried or said she wouldn't stop. Lily seemed to think he felt the same way about her and simply wouldn't accept that he didn't. In the end, the only way to resolve it was to move her out of the area. I can't say I wasn't relieved, by then I'd had enough of the constant drama. The fights and arguments she'd caused here, and regular phone calls from the school about her behaviour were wearing me down. I tried my best, but it didn't make me feel any better when it eventually broke down and she had to be moved onto her fourth placement."

Kevin could hear the raw emotion in every word, she was clearly someone who cared very much and had found the failure to help Lily incredibly painful.

"Did you ever hear what happened to her after she left you?"

Misty nodded, "There's an active fostering grapevine so I did hear about her next placement. Sadly that broke down within two months, not her shortest one, but it's just not going to help someone like Lily settle."

It was hard not to feel for Lily, he thought. Were these the early signs of her becoming so dysfunctional that she'd ended up turning to murder?

"Do you remember why that next placement broke down?"

Misty sighed, "More of the same that I saw and a few new tricks. They had to have her moved as an emergency after she stripped naked and tried to walk into the bathroom when her foster father was in there. Luckily the door was locked and when he saw it turning he had the presence of mind to grab the handle and hold the door closed. If he hadn't he'd have been open to all sorts of allegations, which I'm sure was what Lily was planning."

"It sounds as though Lily wanted to sabotage her placements?"

Misty nodded, "I think that was exactly what she was up to. The social worker told me that when her parents died Lily's older sister applied to take her in but because her accommodation wasn't suitable they had to say no. Lily was apparently furious and I think she tried to cause all her placements to break down in the hopes she'd be sent to live with Andrea."

Kevin tried to put himself in the shoes of a young girl who'd lost her parents and suddenly found herself being dumped off to live in a stranger's home instead of with her older sister. It wasn't surprising that she'd acted out, but he couldn't ignore the similarities between the situation with the teacher and what had happened with Brett.

Piper's face suggested that Steve's visit to her office was as welcome as a bowl of cold sick. She wasn't going to be easy to convince, but if anyone could charm her Steve was pretty sure he could.

"Can you spare me a moment please Ms Daniels?"

She leaned against the door frame blocking him from walking in. Standing in the doorway she glared up at him, "I don't have a moment DS Harding. I'm a busy lady."

Steve shrugged, "Okay, at least I can say I tried.."

Piper stopped him as he turned to leave, "Well, at least tell me what you're here about."

Harding hid his grin as he turned back to face her, "I don't know, I'm getting cold feet about this. If my boss knew I was here behind his back he wouldn't be happy."

That was the golden moment. He saw the interest on her face and knew she was going to bite.

"Then we'd better talk in my office where you won't be overheard."

Bingo, thought Steve as he followed her in and took the seat opposite her desk.

"So, my boss seems to have a massive hard on for your friend Brett, but I'm not seeing it myself. I think he's so focused on Brett that he's missing chasing down other leads and I don't want to end up with egg on my face because of him."

Piper nodded, "It certainly looks that way. Do you have another credible suspect at this point?"

Steve wasn't going to share their investigation with her so he gave her a disarmingly charming smile.

"That's the problem, we're not looking so no one else's name has come up. What I need is a bit more background on Brett so I can use it to steer the DCI away from him."

Piper tapped her pen thoughtfully on her desk as she considered what he was saying.

"Okay, let's say I do talk to you, what's to stop you from using it against Brett instead of helping him?"

Steve shrugged, "If he's as innocent as you say he is then why would anything you tell me be suitable for using against him? Besides, I can't use this conversation as it's unofficial."

Piper nodded, "I can see that working. So, where do you need me to start?"

"How about from the beginning, who knows what might be important? How did you guys meet, how long you've known him, things like that."

Piper reached out and poured herself a glass of water from the jug on her desk, Steve noticed she didn't bother offering him one.

"We met at school and soon became close friends. Brett didn't fit into any of the usual groups so at secondary school he found himself isolated. It was in a science lesson when the teacher paired us up that we got talking for the first time. I stopped thinking of him as the school weirdo and started to enjoy his company. Brett turned out to be amusing, witty, and clever. From that day on, we were inseparable and even after going our separate ways after leaving school we stayed in touch. For a while, we were even flatmates."

"Were you ever anything more than friends?"

Piper gave him a cool look, "Do you not believe that a male and a female can just be friends without anything else going on?"

She didn't wait for him to reply, and Harding got a glimpse of what she was like in court as she put someone under the spotlight on the stand.

"Brett is a good man, he's kind, thoughtful, and has a huge heart. The problem is, he tends to over-inflate his relationships. If he has a spark with a woman, or they seem to click, then he immediately decides she's his soul mate. Brett's been hit hard by the losses, but he's still enough of an optimist to look forward to opening his heart again. It's what makes him such an amazing person and the least likely to kill anyone."

Steve nodded, "What can you tell me about Lily Banks? What was her relationship with Brett like? At this point that's the most damning piece of evidence against Brett, so if we can show it was just the storm in a teacup he says it was we should be able to put it aside.

Piper pulled a face, "She was by far the worst of his girlfriends. Nutty as a fruitcake, and obsessive to the point of stalking him. No matter what anyone said to her, she just wouldn't stop. Absolutely ridiculous. And then, if that wasn't bad enough, she made that assault allegation against him. I was furious."

"Mr Folder did admit to laying his hands on her, and that's something we have to keep in mind when we're investigating. It goes in his favour that she dropped the charges, but it also suggests that maybe she was pressurised into backing off by one of you."

She sighed, "I was starting to think you might be more open-minded than your boss and then you come out with rubbish like that. Brett was very honest with you at his interview, more honest than I'd have advised in fact. He lost his temper and grabbed her, he did not assault her, and he did not say what she claimed he'd said."

Steve's internal detector perked up, those words had played on his mind since he'd seen them in the file. Brett saying "I'll kill you and make it look like an accident," was far too close to what was happening to be ignored.

"More crazy lies DS Harding. There's no way Brett would say anything of the sort."

Steve nodded his agreement while thinking that nothing Piper had told him today had made Brett any less of a suspect. If anything it had solidified Brett as someone who struggled with relationships and his temper.

Had he finally snapped when Lily wouldn't leave him alone and killed her?

DS Harding had added the new information to the whiteboard as he told his DCI about it.

"So, we've got Brett with a definite motive to be behind Lily's disappearance. She was harassing him and he'd got to the end of his tether with her. Then we've got those very prophetic words about coming for her and making it look like an accident. If anything Brett looks more guilty rather than less."

His boss agreed, "He's looking increasingly like the most likely candidate, but all we've got is circumstantial evidence. Nothing really points to him. What did you make of Piper Daniels?"

"She made it clear that she has no reservations in backing up his innocence. Brett can do no wrong in her eyes. She's known him since they were kids, and it would take a lot more than we have to change her opinion of his innocence."

Kevin tapped Lily's name on the board, she was placed in between the victims and suspect's sides as they weren't entirely sure what she was yet.

"What did you make of Lily's history then boss?"

"Her foster mum's description suggests she was a troubled child who would most likely have grown into a damaged woman. We can't discount her at this stage, but my interest is focused on Brett Folder."

The two officers eyed the board in silence and Steve knew they were thinking the same thing.

Was it either Lily or Brett who was responsible for those women's deaths, or were they just accidents and bad luck?

Chapter Nine

Brett was initially reluctant to meet with Ethan, but when Ethan explained to Piper Daniels why he wanted to see her client she was keen for him to engage.

"Brett, this is an excellent way to ensure the police are aware of the trauma caused by your losses. Dr Quinn's notes will be admissible in court, and it'll help us more than the prosecution. I'll sit in of course, we can't risk allowing questions that could be used against you without you having legal representation."

Ethan hadn't been entirely pleased with Piper's presence. Not because he was planning to do or say anything that would jeopardise Brett's rights, but because having someone else in the room often meant a patient wouldn't be as honest and open with their answers. He'd have to make the best of it, but it wasn't ideal. Brett fidgeted anxiously as Ethan sat down and got out his notebook and pen.

Tugging his cuffs down he picked at imaginary lint on his clothes, "Where do we start Dr Quinn?"

Ethan gave Brett his most reassuring smile, "This isn't meant to be painful Mr. Folder, the complete opposite in fact. You've been through so much recently and this is just to ascertain how you're coping and if you need any additional support."

Brett was nodding, but Piper shot Ethan a suspicious look, "Usually I would be the one to arrange an appointment like this so excuse me if I appear cynical as to why the police are suddenly interested in Brett's welfare."

"Considering how often the police have been in hot water for not taking someone's mental health into account it's been decided that in cases such as Brett's, they'll be more proactive with arranging that support."

Piper seemed slightly mollified by his explanation, but not enough to leave them alone to talk. Settling herself more comfortably into her seat she ensured he knew she wasn't going anywhere. Ethan turned his attention to Brett, he may as well try to get as much out of this as possible regardless of Piper's interference.

"I usually find it's best to start at the beginning. What can you tell me about your relationship with Ruby Stevens?"

Brett blinked furiously, he clearly didn't feel entirely comfortable but Ethan sat quietly and waited for him to start.

"I met Ruby at a music gig, we were both dragged along by friends and weren't really enjoying the band. We hit it off and exchanged numbers and it went from there. She was fun and made me laugh at a time when I was trying to cope with Lily's unwanted attention. I was worried that Ruby would drop me after the incident with Lily at the pub, but instead, she just shrugged it off and we carried on as before. I thought she was my soul mate and we'd be together longer term. I could see marriage and children in our future, but then it was all taken away from me. I'm sure you must think it was unnaturally quick for me to move on with someone else within a few months, I know Piper did. If you'd known Mandy you'd have understood though. She was so full of life and optimism, even at a time when the country was in the middle of something so terrible."

Ethan noted that when Brett rubbed his eyes it was to give the impression of wiping away tears, but there was no evidence he'd been crying when he dropped his hands.

"You and Mandy were living together at the time of her accident weren't you?"

Brett nodded, "Maybe the pandemic made us more hasty. There's nothing like a life-threatening virus to prompt you to live for the day, but I like to think we'd have moved in together anyway. It was a terrible blow to lose her so suddenly a year after I'd lost my Ruby, and until I met Stella on New Year's Eve I thought I'd be alone forever. Stella was miserable, she was grieving the end of a relationship in the same way I was grieving Mandy's loss and it drew us together. After her it was Lucy. Lucy was more a bit of fun than a serious relationship, she made me smile, and I enjoyed her company. I thought I'd break the curse by going abroad with her for Valentine's but she too suffered a tragic accident. The worst was probably Cara, an accident is one thing, but to learn that someone murdered her like that was horrible."

Brett ran a finger under his eye as though he was catching a stray tear, "I can only think it must've been a case of mistaken identity. Cara was such a kind and responsible woman I can't see her being involved with someone who'd stab her in cold blood like that."

It was interesting how Brett gave the impression of grief and loss, but Ethan noticed there was something lacking in his tone, and his expression wasn't quite right either. It could be shock, with the amount of trauma he'd had there could easily be some disassociation, but the other explanation was that Brett was trying to mimic the right emotions rather than feeling them.

"What can you tell me about Lily Banks?"

Her name seemed to sit on the table like a physical presence, Brett went pale and Piper glared at Ethan.

"Do we really have to talk about her? It was a traumatic time for Brett and each time he has to relive it he's retraumatised."

Ethan noticed her use of the right terms and hid a smile at her cleverness, not that it'd put him off, but he always admired ingenuity.

"I appreciate how difficult it must be, but if we're going to get a full picture of the impact on Brett we need to look at the relationship that appears to have triggered everything."

Brett glanced at Piper and when she dipped her head in agreement he reluctantly began.

"Lily and I met on a night out with friends, she was on the peripherals of the group and I felt out of place so we just seemed to drift to each other. We exchanged numbers and although she was quick to text me I didn't sense anything was untoward with her. Our first Valentine's Day was less than a week after we'd met, we'd only been on a couple of dates but she made a huge deal out of it. I brought her a card and a stuffed bear, but I was embarrassed when she produced a huge card embossed with "For My Boyfriend." Lily also got me several expensive gifts and it all felt a bit uncomfortable. Piper will tell you that I'm someone who likes to avoid confrontation and unpleasantness, so I just got myself through the rest of the evening. The plan had been to end things soon after, but Lily wouldn't take the hint. No matter how I tried to pull away from her she just kept messaging and showing up as though there was nothing wrong. As I told the officers, Christmas was a turning point and I realised that I needed to be clearer with her. I finally ended it in February 2019, but she continued to stalk and harass me. It got even worse when I met Ruby, Lily was incandescent with rage and stepped up her campaign. I expect you're already aware of the incident where I lost my temper and grabbed her and then her lies about me threatening her life."

Ethan had been taking notes, "And when did she stop bothering you Mr Folder? The police have struggled to find her whereabouts and it would be helpful to know when you last saw or heard from her."

Brett shrugged and raised his eyes as he thought about it, "I'd say it was after the incident where she accused me of assaulting her and threatening to kill her. She stopped showing up at the house and then she dropped the charges and I didn't see her again. I've always assumed she met someone else and moved her obsession to them. Poor bastard whoever he was."

Not wanting to push too hard in case Brett or Piper suspected him of having too much of an interest, Ethan didn't comment. He did, however, note the query in his head.

If Lily had met someone else that didn't explain why she'd vanished so effectively. Not many people managed to disappear completely in this day and age. Who managed without a mobile phone, access to banking, and without using their national insurance number?

Piper glanced at her expensive watch before tapping the face as though to draw attention to it.

"I think that's enough for one day Dr Quinn."

Ethan nodded his agreement, her words suggested that he might get another bite on the cherry if he played his cards right and didn't push too hard now.

"Yes, I wouldn't want to cause Mr Folder any additional distress. I'll also leave my card, if you feel in need of my support please don't hesitate to call me."

Standing up and packing away his belongings Ethan glanced at Brett and Piper to try and read their expressions. Brett looked relieved to see him go, but Piper's expression was difficult to read. Her eyes were lowered, but her shoulders were tense and rigid suggesting stress and anxiety.

The question was, what did she have to be anxious about? Was she concerned that Ethan would find out the truth of what her friend had done?

"She's definitely very protective of him. Is that because she's his lawyer or his friend? I'm not sure if it's either or if perhaps it's a combination of both."

Ethan had called them earlier and arranged for them all to meet up at his house again. The two officers sat on the sofa while Ethan took his favourite armchair with his cat, Eric, on his lap. In the last few months, he'd got on with unpacking and organising and the place finally resembled an actual home rather than a place he'd just landed up in.

Kevin listened with interest to his feedback, leaning forward in his seat and taking in every detail. Ethan found DCI Greggs to be a man who followed his gut and didn't quit on a case no matter how long it took to get to the bottom of it.

"So, where does this leave us in regards to who is the most likely suspect?"

It felt like a rhetorical question, Ethan thought. It wasn't as though they could be definite without anything more than gut feelings and what he could glean from such a short conversation.

"My early thoughts are that Brett's masking, but what he's masking I can't be a hundred percent sure. All I can say is that he's definitely hiding something from me. His emotional range was a little off too. That could be down to shock and disassociation caused by all the trauma, or it could be because he's a cold psychopath who knows how to play-act the right responses. He seems to have a way with women. What with not having a shortage of girlfriends, his friend Piper seems to hang off his every word too. That's another potential red flag, psychopaths are often described as superficially charming. There's also the way he jumps impulsively from one relationship to another so quickly."

Ethan shrugged, "I'd need a few more sessions with him to get a real reading. Plus I'd need to see him one to one and not with his lawyer friend breathing down my neck."

Kevin waggled his hand at Ethan, "Not sure how likely that is Doc. So, we've got Brett at the top of the list still, but Lily is a close second. That or he's bumped her off too and buried her so deep no one's found her yet."

Chapter Ten

DCI Greggs looked up at the block of flats that was Lily's last known home. Four flats made it a small block and it looked well cared for from the outside. Checking the intercom system he found the one with the registered building owner's name and pressed it. A harsh, husky voice demanded to know who he was.

"Yeah, police? Fucks sake. Stay there I'll be right out, I want to see ID before I let you in the block."

The short, skinny woman with the mop of unruly blonde hair looked to be in her 70s. A cigarette clung to her bottom lip and bobbed up and down as she spoke. Joan Clem, ex-landlady for Lily Banks, and hopefully someone who could tell Kevin where she'd gone when she'd moved out.

After scrutinising their ID for what seemed to be forever, she finally jerked her head to indicate they could come in. Leading them along the hall she kicked open the door at the furthest end and let them into her flat. It was reasonably clean, but cluttered, with numerous photos and ornaments that lined every surface and walls.

"Which one of my lot has done something this time? If it's another cannabis grow then show me the warrant and I'll give you the spare key. No need to smash the door through like you did last time, it's just another headache for me to deal with. I don't need that shit at my age."

Kevin shook his head, "It's not a warrant or a grow that we're here about. We'd like to know about your ex-tenant, Lily Banks."

The woman pulled a sour face, "That little madam. Fucked off without a word the day her rent was due. January 2020 it was, end of the month. Never saw or heard a thing from her. Left all her shit in the flat too. Who do you think had to sort that out? Muggins here, that's who."

"When did you last see her? Do you know where she was going?"

Joan sniffed, "I heard her in the hall so I went out to remind her that her rent was due the next day. She was just going out and promised to send it over to me. Said she was going to see that boyfriend of hers, Brett something or other. She made this sickly love face whenever she talked about him, all dreamy and gooey about the guy. I remember thinking she'd soon change her tune once she got to know him properly."

That made Kevin's ears perk up, "What made you say that? Did you meet him?"

"Yeah I met him a couple of times, but only briefly. It wasn't about him personally, just men in general. Once the rose tint dropped from her eyes she'd see him for what he was. Same as all the others, full of crap and untrustworthy. I didn't really get to know him, I just caught a glimpse of him in passing, and one time she introduced us. He didn't seem keen to chat, all eager to get up to her flat and away from the nosy old bird downstairs. Good looking bloke, but one of those that seem a bit too polished and charming if you know what I mean."

Interesting, thought Kevin, was she really going to meet Brett that night? From what Brett had told them she'd made that accusation against him and then dropped it. He said he hadn't seen her again and thought she'd met someone else.

"Did she say it was Brett she was meeting specifically?"

Joan thought for a moment, "It was a while ago now, but now you ask I'm thinking maybe not. It seems to ring a bell that she just said she was going to see her boyfriend and maybe I assumed it was Brett because that's who she'd been seeing."

"What did you think of her?"

The little bird like woman shrugged her thin shoulders, "She was alright. She paid her rent on time, didn't make a noise, and was friendly enough when I spoke to her. I thought she was going to be a nice long-term tenant until she did a bunk on me."

Steve added the information to the whiteboard, "So, do we think Lily was off to indulge in her favourite hobby of watching Brett that night, or that he really was going to meet up with her?"

Kevin nodded, "I'd reckon it was more likely that she was off to stalk him, and if that's the case then maybe Brett saw her out there and lost his rag again. The difference was, this time he went all the way and ended up killing her."

"That also begs the question, is the harassment story true anyway? We only have Brett and Piper's word for it. No reports to the police, and no one else seems to have seen anything."

Steve had a good point, Kevin conceded. They didn't know for a fact that the stalking allegation was even true. What they did know was that Lily had made a report about an assault that she'd later dropped. They also knew that at least one of Brett's girlfriends was definitely murdered even if the others had been ruled an accident.

"What if she'd found someone else by then? A new man that she was obsessing over and he did something to her. The other possibility is that she's living under the radar, or even moved abroad and we're barking up the wrong tree entirely."

Steve frowned, "If that's the case boss, we'd be able to take Lily off the list and focus all our attention on Brett or a person as yet unknown to us. I've got a contact who can check the flights and see if a Lily Banks flew anywhere around that time."

Kevin nodded his agreement, "That's your job allocated. I'm going to keep digging in Brett and Lily's pasts to try and find someone else to speak to.

We need more background because if either of them are responsible for this there'll have been a sign or an incident that points to them. Brett can't be summed up by just one friend, there has to be other people and not just Piper."

Chapter Eleven

A trawl through Brett's social media led Kevin to a new name. Lauren Andrews, the girlfriend he'd dated before Lily Banks, and from his searches one that appeared to be alive and kicking. Kevin was sitting in Ethan's cosy living room so he turned the laptop around and showed him what he'd found.

The doctor leaned in for a closer look, "He's definitely got a type, this one looks very similar to the others. Not that having a type indicates he's a killer, but it's certainly something to add to the database of things we know about him."

Kevin nodded, "I'd like a little chat with Miss Andrews. Since she's one of the only women we've come across who hasn't disappeared or died she might have some useful information for us."

He eyed Ethan, "I wouldn't mind taking you along if you can spare the time? You could give me a read on her and anything she tells us will help build your background on Brett."

Ethan grinned, "I'd love to. This case has really sucked me in and I have to admit I'm quite eager to try and come up with some answers now. Lucky for you, I'm on leave and Stella's away visiting a friend so I'm at a loose end. As I'm easily bored and my job is my main interest in life then I'm all yours."

Kevin glanced at his watch, no matter that most people used their phones as timekeepers now he preferred a real time piece. Besides, there was also a sentimentality to it as his beloved Alison had brought it for him on what turned out to be their last Christmas.

"It's not too late to do a drop in now if you're up for it?"

Ethan was already getting his wallet and keys, "Sounds perfect."

Lauren Andrews hadn't let them into her flat until she'd fully scrutinised them and their ID badges through the ring doorbell camera. Only once she'd satisfied herself they were genuine and safe did she open the door. Kevin gave her what he hoped was a reassuring smile. Lauren was a short, curvy woman with wide frightened eyes and worry lines across her forehead.

She'd quietly offered them a drink and once they were sat around the table in the kitchen she'd waited to hear what they wanted from her.

"Thank you for seeing us Miss Andrews. We were hoping you could tell us about your ex-partner, Brett Folder. It's nothing to worry about, it's just a background check regarding the unfortunate death of his current partner."

Lauren looked startled, "Gosh, that was a long time ago, I'm not sure how much help I can be. What sort of information are you looking for?"

"Let's start with why the relationship ended, was it on good terms?"

The woman shrugged, "I guess it wasn't really acrimonious, but what break-up isn't painful on some level? Brett and I had differing ideas of where the relationship was going and as those ideas weren't compatible, and it wasn't something we could compromise on, we decided to go our separate ways."

There was something rehearsed about the way she told it, as though it was a story she'd learned by heart. Kevin was pretty sure there was more to it, but it wouldn't be helpful if he tried to push too hard, too soon.

"Can I ask what it was that you couldn't resolve?"

Although his words had been gentle and carefully thought out she ducked her head as though they were physically painful.

"If you must have the difficult details, Brett was very gungho about the idea of us moving in together. We'd only been together for a short time, a few months, but he was determined we were going to be a forever thing. "What's the point in waiting? Life's too short to put things off." That was his way of trying to persuade me, but all it did was frighten me more. In the end, we were arguing about it almost every time we got together, and I just felt it was unhealthy for both of us. He was terribly upset at the time, but I was glad to see he'd moved on when he met someone else. Lily, I think her name was."

Kevin could see she wasn't comfortable with sharing such personal details, but he knew this was his best opportunity to find out more about Brett.

"We were also hoping you'd be able to tell us about his family history. Friends, family, anyone close to him."

Lauren seemed more comfortable with this, "Brett's parents don't live in the country. They haven't for years so he was raised by his Aunt, Beryl Stratford, and she was the closest he had to a parent that I knew of. His family is very wealthy so he's never wanted for anything financially, but it always felt he'd been left very short on the emotional side. Maybe that was why he was so eager for us to move in together. I guess he might have been trying to create the family that he'd missed out on growing up."

This was definitely helpful stuff as far as building a picture of Brett was concerned, "Did you ever meet his Aunt? What was she like?"

"She was quite austere. I wasn't especially comfortable with visiting her, she'd virtually ignore me while I was there and she wasn't overly affectionate to Brett either. If I had to pick a word to describe her I'd say cold."

"Did you get along with his friend Piper?"

Lauren waggled a hand to demonstrate that it was an up-and-down relationship, "I take it Piper is still around then? She was his best friend from school, she wasn't awful to me, but I always felt she didn't approve of me. Between Piper and Brett's Aunt, it felt as though they were saying I wasn't good enough. It made me feel inadequate. Piper tried to talk to me about Brett's desire for us to move in together. She seemed to feel I was letting him down to start with, but eventually, I felt as though she got where I was coming from."

Curling her hands around her mug of coffee Lauren flicked her gaze from one man to the other.

"I'm not entirely comfortable talking about Brett behind his back like this. I don't have anything terrible to say about him, he didn't hit me or abuse me, he just wanted too much too soon."

Kevin nodded, "Thank you, Miss Andrews, that's really helpful. We weren't looking for you to tell us anything awful, and we do appreciate that this must've been difficult."

Lauren nodded, the haunted look in her eye bothered Kevin but he wasn't sure what else to say to try and find out what it was. He didn't feel as though it was Brett connected, but if it was then they needed to hear it.

Ethan must've noticed that the DCI had stalled because he leaned forward and gently asked her about the elephant in the room.

Lauren made an insightful point when she said that Brett may be desperately seeking to replace the love and affection that was missing from his childhood."

Kevin turned the key in the ignition, "Then let's head straight over there."

Finding Beryl's address hadn't taken long. She didn't live far from Lauren, but the area was still far removed from Lauren's very basic accommodation.

Beryl lived in a large sprawling country house set in acres of well-tended grounds. The floodlights came on as they detected Kevin's car and the crunch of the gravel gave an auditory warning of their approach which was probably why the front door swung open before they'd got much further than climbing out of the car.

The woman in the doorway was backlit by dim hall lighting. Her grey hair was pulled back in a tight bun that stretched her wrinkled skin. Her cold eyes watched them as they walked toward her. Kevin had already got his warrant card out and she read it silently before giving them a terse nod.

"You'd better come inside I suppose."

There was no offer of a drink as they took a seat, "What can I do for you both? As you can imagine it's not a regular occurrence that the police visit my home of an evening, or at any time for that matter."

Kevin took the lead, "I'm not sure if you're aware, but your nephew's girlfriend was sadly killed recently. As part of our investigation into her death, we need to carry out background checks on everyone involved with the woman."

Beryl snorted, "Really? Don't take me for a fool young man. I'm perfectly aware that as this woman's boyfriend, you've placed my nephew in the number one suspect spot. It's the typical small-minded, narrow thinking that I've come to expect from the police. Piper has filled me in on your harassment of my nephew and your total lack of respect that he's grieving."

Kevin decided to ignore the digs, "Did you ever meet Cara Edwards?"

Brett's Aunt snorted again, "Of course I met her. My nephew introduces me to all of his girlfriends, he values my opinion."

"And what was your opinion?"

"Yet another insipid, yes woman. Just my nephew's type. He's unable to cope with a strong partner so he seeks out those who bolster his fragile ego. I'd always hoped he'd eventually get together with Piper, with her pushing him in the right direction he'd make so much more of himself. Instead, Brett's attracted to losers. It's something I've had to come to terms with, unfortunately. That and his flighty approach to life. Constantly changing jobs and daydreaming. He's just like his mother."

"So, has anything ever happened between Brett and Piper that made you think they'd get together?"

Beryl shook her head, "Don't be ridiculous, haven't you listened to a word I've been saying? Piper isn't his type and I doubt Brett would ever be hers either."

"How old was Brett when he came to live with you?"

Beryl sighed impatiently, "About six or seven. I'm his father's sister and when he was made a decent job offer abroad it was a choice between boarding school and me. Brett had always been an oversensitive child so it was felt that being sent away to school wouldn't be a suitable option."

She snorted, "I remember the day they left him here. He was bawling his eyes out and clutching his mother's legs like a little limpet and she was no better. Instead of calming things down she was snivelling and begging my brother not to leave him here. Luckily my brother stuck to his guns, I'm sure I've given Brett a more grounded upbringing than his parents could've."

Kevin could picture the small boy clutching onto his mother before being left here with this cold, unfeeling woman. He shuddered at the thought.

"Did he see a lot of them after they left? Are they still in contact?"

Beryl's face showed a glimmer of pain, "They died when Brett was eleven in an accident. They took a turning too fast and went over the cliff edge and died instantly. Brake failure apparently. Just before that, his mother had been in touch to say they were settled and coming to collect Brett to live with them again. He was devastated as you can imagine."

Standing up she fixed Kevin and Ethan with a hard stare, "And that's all I've got for you. I'm really not comfortable dredging up Brett's past for no good reason and I suggest you start looking for a real suspect. That's unless you want Piper to lodge a formal complaint for harassment against you."

Beryl had led them to the front door as she delivered her lecture. Throwing it open she flapped her hand suggesting they hurry up and leave her house. Kevin paused in the doorway, "Mrs Stratford, one last question. Did you meet Lily Banks? She appears to be missing and we've been unable to find any evidence of her whereabouts over the last few years?"

Brett's aunt stared at Kevin in silence for a moment, "I met Lily a few times, sadly she appears to have been mentally unstable. My nephew told me all about the stalking and harassment. I urged him to take Piper's advice and go down an official route to stop her, but Brett was too embarrassed to admit her behaviour was upsetting him."

Kevin gave her a sharp nod before following Ethan outside. As they pulled away he glanced into the rearview mirror and saw Beryl was still standing on her doorstep watching them leave.

Back at Ethan's house, Kevin nursed his cup of coffee, "What were your thoughts on Aunty Beryl?"

"I'd say Lauren's description didn't quite go far enough. She didn't seem to have much affection for her nephew, did she? I especially cringed at her description of Brett's exes as losers."

Ethan looked thoughtful, "I'd say we got a fair bit from Aunty Beryl that helps our profile. There's his preferences when it comes to girlfriends and the type of upbringing I imagine he'd have had. When you consider the emotional and physical distance from his parents and how cold his substitute caregiver is then he'll have missed out on the usual love, affection, and confidence boosts that a child needs. Imagine the tragedy of thinking you were going back to live with your parents only to lose them like that. Brett must've been crushed, and I don't see Aunty Beryl providing much comfort either."

Kevin considered what Ethan was saying, "But does that make the man a killer? And don't forget, we're not just talking once either, there's the five who are definitely dead, and if we count Lily that's six. Can he actually be a serial killer?"

Steepling his fingers Ethan took a moment to re-read Kevin's notes, "I don't like to make snap diagnoses based on secondhand information, but I wouldn't rule him out."

Kevin pulled his coat on, "I'll pass all of this on to Harding in the morning. I don't think I've said it yet, but thanks for this Ethan. I've had to work on this case alone for so long it's been a great boost to have your input as well as having Steve on board too. I honestly think we're going to get to the bottom of this, even though right now it feels as though we're as far away as I was at the start."

Chapter Twelve

DCI Greggs wanted to stamp his feet in frustration, any sense of optimism he'd felt earlier had vanished at the news that Steve hadn't found any sign that Lily had left the country.

"Maybe she used a fake passport boss? I've had my contact searching for Lily Banks, but if she was under another name it wouldn't flag up."

Kevin shook his head, "And how would your run-of-the-mill citizen have access to someone who could create a fake passport of the quality needed to get by the type of security we've got at the borders? I'd love to believe it, if true it'd tie everything up in a nice neat bow, but it's just beyond the realms of possibility. We've got no intel to suggest that Lily would've had access to a counterfeiter that could provide her with a false passport. Not only that, but I can't believe she'd have the money to pay for it even if she knew where to go."

Harding shrugged, "I know, even as I was saying it I thought about how unlikely it was. I just thought I'd throw it out there so we can scrub it off as a possibility."

"This information means we can assume that she didn't fly off to sunnier climes. Which leaves us with the original assumption that she's here in the country somewhere, the question is, is she dead or alive? Alive would put her on our suspect list, dead would add her to Brett's alleged tally of victims."

He paused while he thought out the options, "We can either keep looking, and let's be honest it'll be like finding a needle in a haystack, or we bring Brett back in for questioning."

Harding grinned, "I like door number two best boss."

Kevin sent the uniforms over to pick Brett up. He spent the time waiting for him to arrive getting the interview room ready. Heating set so it was a little chilly, but not so much that he or his brief could raise concerns. He pushed the table snug against the wall to give the psychological impression of being trapped. It was all in the little things. Unnerving the suspect just enough that you could push them into talking to you.

Brett inevitably requested Piper be brought in as his brief, and as she hadn't been at his house when he was arrested Brett had to wait in his cell cooling his heels until she showed up. Most worryingly the uniforms reported that whilst Piper wasn't present in his home, another woman had been. It appeared Brett had moved on to a new woman already. It gave Kevin a feeling that he'd been right to move when he had, if he was right about Brett he may just have saved that woman's life.

It was another two hours until Kevin finally had Brett and Piper in his specially arranged interview room. He hid a grin as she saw Piper rub her arms against the mild chill.

"Can you turn the heating up please DCI Greggs?"

Kevin frowned as though puzzled, "I'm not cold, are you DS Harding?"

Steve shook his head, "Not me boss, I'm warm as toast, I was going to ask you to turn it down a notch."

Piper glared at them both, "My client is entitled to be interviewed in a room that's of ambient temperature and we all know this room isn't warm enough to meet that requirement."

"DS Harding, can you go and ask one of the uniforms to find the thermostat and turn the heating up a bit please?"

Kevin knew Harding would pass on the message and that the PC would also know to take his sweet time about doing it. By now Piper had turned her attention to the table's position and from the wrinkling of her upturned nose she was finding his setup not to her taste either.

"There's plenty of room for the table to be further in the middle and not rammed up against the wall where Brett has to brush shoulders with the brickwork."

DCI Greggs shrugged, "I wouldn't know Miss Daniels. I just picked the first available room and this is how it was laid out. I'm sorry if it isn't to your liking but I didn't have time to redecorate or move the furnishings about."

Piper's face said she'd seen right through him, but he knew she wouldn't bother fighting a losing battle about it.

"Fine, let's just get on with it shall we?"

Just then Harding came back into the room and Kevin started the tape. Recording the names of all present he started by throwing a photo of Lily onto the table.

"I find it very strange that we can't find this young woman. What I also find odd is that she was very present right up until she made those assault accusations against you. Lily appears to have dropped the charges and then vanished without a trace. Is she frightened of you Mr Folder? Is that why she's gone into hiding?"

Brett's mouth was a thin, grim line, "No comment."

Piper examined her nails as though the answers to everything lay in her cuticles, she gave a delicate yawn in Kevin's direction.

"Boring. So very boring. Do you have anything else? If not I suggest you may as well let my client go."

Ignoring her as though she hadn't spoken Kevin kept his eyes on Brett, "We spoke to your Aunty Beryl. Tough old bird isn't she?"

Brett glared back and gritted his teeth, "No comment."

Kevin nodded as though Brett had joined in the conversation, "Must've been hard living with someone who doesn't seem to be very affectionate, especially after losing your parents at such a young age. You were eleven weren't you?"

That little nugget had hit home, Brett's eyes narrowed, but he managed to bite back whatever comment he'd had on the tip of his tongue.

"No comment."

"We've got a search warrant for your property Mr Folder, what are we going to find there?"

Brett turned his head away and looked at the wall, "No comment."

"Sounds as though you had a lonely childhood Mr Folder, and your Aunty Beryl seems to think there's something lacking in the type of woman you pick up with."

Piper straightened in her chair, "Is there a question in there or is it just a supposition like the rest of this nonsense?"

"If you'd prefer a question, here's one. Who's the new woman you've taken up with Mr Folder? Should we be concerned for her safety? It seems it's a bit of a death wish getting involved with you."

Brett's face paled and a nerve twitched next to his eye, and Piper shot him a sharp look that suggested she hadn't known about this additional bit of information. From the expression on her face, it seemed she wasn't too pleased either.

"No comment. My love life is nothing to do with any of you."

The addition on the end made Kevin smile, he'd managed to goad Brett past the no-comment response, and it was just a matter of keeping the pressure on now. A few more decent questions and the man would crumble giving Kevin exactly what he needed.

His moment of joy was interrupted when a uniform knocked and then entered the room. Announcing the newcomer's presence he turned to him with a huff of annoyance.

"PC Marsh, can't you see I'm in the middle of an interview? This had better be urgent."

Kevin was hoping the interruption was due to the team having found something of interest in Brett's house.

"The inspector would like to speak to you urgently, he's outside in the corridor."

PC Marsh was obviously ensuring that Kevin didn't say anything untoward loud enough to be overheard. Announcing a pause to the tape he pushed his chair back and walked out of the door. The inspector was leaning against the wall, his face grim and irritated.

"I didn't sign off on that warrant Greggs. I won't ask how you managed to get it but just know I'm pissed off about it. What I can do something about is you leaving us open for a harassment complaint. Let that man go immediately, and you'd better hope the search team turns up something of value or it's your head on the block."

Shit, shit, shit.

If he let Brett go now he'd lose his advantage, but he couldn't hold him in breach of a direct order to let him go. He'd have to play it clever and make it seem as though he had an ace up his sleeve and it was all part of his plan.

"Yes sir."

The inspector gave him a long look in response to his tone so Kevin kept his expression neutral until the Inspector turned on his heel and marched away. Going back into the room he turned the tape back on and reannounced all the participants. Piper looked smug and he wondered if she'd guessed some of the conversation he'd just had.

"I'm going to bail you again Mr Folder. You're unable to return home until the search is complete so please let the front desk know where we can find you."

Piper smirked and he wondered if it was her or the Aunt who'd pulled the strings necessary to get the inspector's ear. No matter, if the search turned up any evidence he'd have Brett back in here so fast his feet wouldn't touch the ground. No one could stop him if he found something concrete and all he could hope was that a piece of evidence would show up.

Ethan had come in handy once again, he'd managed to find a social worker who was willing to talk about Lily off the record.

"Harriet Althrop retired about two years ago, she's a firm, no-nonsense sort, but she does care about her charges more deeply than you'd think on the surface. Harry's old school and if she thinks what she knows is important she'll have no problem sharing."

The doctor set up the meeting at Harriet's home and that's where Kevin was currently sitting. The retired social worker's living room was sparsely furnished leaving Kevin with no choice but to take the armchair that was thick with cat hair. The culprit, Mr Tibbs, stared malevolently at him from his perch on the top of a bookcase.

As Ethan described, Harriet was straight to the point, "Lily Banks. She was one of my caseload that I found hard to forget after she left our care. I'm not sure how well you know the system, but unless a young person is going onto our leaving care team we tend to close them out at eighteen. Far too young in my opinion, if you were in your birth family you wouldn't be out on your ear at that age so we're disadvantaging our young people from the start."

Kevin could see the frustration that Harriet still felt about the system, but he couldn't help but agree with her. A high percentage of the offenders he dealt with had spent time in the care system.

"We've been trying to find Lily to speak to her about an ex-partner. I can't go into details about the case but we need to eliminate Lily as either a victim or perpetrator."

Harriet nodded knowingly, "From the start Lily was attracted to unsuitable men. They were always older and she'd become so obsessed she'd create a relationship with them in her head. I can see from her notes that her social worker tried to address this with her a number of times, but Lily took no notice. This behaviour saw her moved from placement to placement which I'm sure led to even more disruption and distress for her. Lily was already angry when she was bought into care and all of this didn't help."

Kevin checked his notes, "We were told her parents died suddenly when she was thirteen, I'd imagine this being her first contact with social services she found it all very overwhelming."

Harriet frowned, "Who said it was her first contact with us? Lily was on the at risk register for a number of years before her parents died. Her older sister, Andrea, made some allegations that both parents were using drugs and neglecting them. Lily would've just been born at the time, Andrea was a lot older than her. Her records show we made an unannounced visit and found the home to be in a terrible state. Lily and Andrea were removed. We managed to find a sibling placement so we kept them together until the parents improved enough for them to be returned home. We monitored them for a while, but by the time Andrea had left home our involvement had ended. We got involved again when their parents died in a house fire. Luckily Lily was away on a sleepover at the time otherwise she'd have perished too. The poor child was devastated. Andrea put her hand up to take Lily in, and while we generally prefer family fostering unfortunately she didn't have the room where she lived or the financial resources. Lily was incredibly bitter and angry as you can imagine and made it her life's work to try and sabotage every placement in the hope that we'd relent and hand her over to her sister."

It was hard to hear, thought Kevin, the poor kid hadn't had a great start and now she was either a damaged woman killing other women, or she'd been murdered herself.

"Were there ever any further discussions about Lily going to live with her sister?"

Harriet shook her head, "I've looked at the notes and it seems that once Lily was placed in foster care we had no further contact from Andrea. Lily was working on a poor plan if she thought her behaviour would get her the chance to live with her older sister."

"What was the last contact that social services had with Lily?"

"Her records show that we ensured she was in education, had a place to live, and was financially able to support herself and then we closed her case."

Harriet closed her eyes for a moment, "I know exactly how that sounds and I'm not defending the system. Far from it, I think it's appalling, but we do the best we can with the resources we have. Lily was failed by the system, she was left alone and unsupported and I'd imagine she was still festering with frustration and bitterness. She hadn't had any mental health input about the obsessive behaviour either. The waiting list for child mental health services is ridiculous. Lily was on that list for so long that she didn't see anyone before she was closed at eighteen. Maybe with that input, she'd have been a more able adult, but instead, I can imagine she was still damaged when she was left to make the best of things."

Kevin could see Harriet was fighting back tears which she brusquely brushed away with a balled up hand. Standing up she made it clear she'd said as much as she could.

"If that's all DCI Greggs?"

Kevin, grateful for her help and not wanting to upset her further, also stood.

"Thank you Ms Althrop, it's much appreciated."

She nodded but looked lost in the bad memories of the past as she showed him to the door.

PC Marsh was grinning from ear to ear when he burst into Kevin's office.

"Good news boss. The search team has found something we think you'll be very interested in."

Crossing his fingers under the table Kevin waited to hear the answer. PC Marsh dropped a pack of evidence bags onto the desk. Each photo was individually sealed away and Kevin flicked through them all, his grin widening with each image.

This was exactly what he'd been hoping for, Brett'd have a hard time explaining these away, he thought. What had once been snapshots of Brett and the woman in question were now more of an expression of hate.

Every woman's face had been scribbled out with a hand so heavy the photo had torn.

Having seen PC Marsh go in Harding had come into the office. Leaning over Kevin's shoulder he winced.

"That's a lot of hate right there. Do we think Brett was keeping these to remember the women after he offed them?"

Kevin shrugged, "Who knows what goes on in a mind as sick as his. Those poor women and that's only the ones we know about. I can't help but wonder if there's other missing girlfriends out there."

Steve winced at the thought, "And I guess we're taking Lily off the suspect list and adding her to the victim one now?"

"I'm losing hope of finding her alive, after talking to that social worker I was starting to see her as the perpetrator again, but this changes things. I was also hoping to get a chance to speak to her older sister in case Lily was hiding out with her. Sadly, I think it's more likely we're going to be turning up a body instead."

Pushing those dark thoughts aside and giving Harding a grin, he picked up his keys and made sure he had his cuffs in his pocket.

"Let's go and pick up Brett Folder, he's got a lot of explaining to do this time."

Chapter Thirteen

According to the front desk Brett had given his temporary bail address as Piper's place.

Kevin pulled a face, "That's all we need, bulldog Piper breathing down our necks about unfairly harassing her client."

Harding huffed, "Let's not forget making sure it reaches the inspector's ears again in the hopes we can be pressurised into letting Brett go."

"Not this time. This time we've got him on the hook and he's not squirming off it."

When they pulled up outside Kevin could see a strip of light between the curtains in the room next to the front door. By the time they'd walked up onto the porch though, he could also hear raised voices.

They were too far away to hear what was being said, but Kevin knew the sound of someone being really pissed off when he heard it.

"Harding, sneak around the back while I try to get closer. If you find a way in take it and try and find out what's going on in there."

Steve nodded, "Sounds to me like the lawyer lady isn't keen on her client right now."

He slipped into the darkness and disappeared around the side of the house. Kevin crouched down where he wouldn't be seen if anyone looked out of a window. On the opposite side of the front door, he found a window that wasn't latched up like the others. Giving it a gentle push he managed to make a gap just big enough for him to get through. Dropping down onto the deep pile carpet he felt his way to the internal door and out into the hall. From here the voices were clearer and he could pick up what was going on.

"What the fuck are you doing with another woman already Brett? Can't you see how it must look to the police?"

Brett's voice came back with a sharp snappy retort, "I'm in love with Fran for your information and I don't give a shit how it looks to anyone else."

"You're an idiot, a bloody idiot Brett. You'll just end up back in the same situation as you were when you were with that weirdo Lily"

Brett's voice sounded irritated, "Just drop it, Piper, if it wasn't for those ridiculous bail conditions I'd leave and get a hotel. I don't need this crap right now."

Piper's voice rose, "You don't need this crap? Oh yes, it's all about you isn't it?"

Kevin grinned to himself, he hated to break up a decent argument like this one but he was also pretty eager to get Brett back down the station. They'd pick up where he'd left off earlier and this time he had the evidence he needed to really break Brett once and for all.

His smile faded as he heard a third, female, voice, "Interesting conversation. Perhaps you'd like to repeat what you were saying about Lily just now?"

Piper let out a scream, "Shit, is that a knife? Who the hell are you?"

That was a question that Kevin would like answering too, it couldn't be Lily if Piper was asking who she was, or could it? The problem was he couldn't tell where anyone in the room was, if he busted in now without backup he could find himself right in the firing line. Leaning his head against the door he listened to see if he could work out what was going on in there.

"I want to know what happened to my sister Lily. One of you knows exactly where she is and if no one tells me I'll start cutting pieces off you until you talk. Don't think I won't do it either. You have no idea what I'm capable of."

There was a metallic click, a familiar sound to Kevin who recognised that the woman was handcuffing Brett and Piper.

"Now, whose going first? One of you knows what happened to her. Was it you Brett? Did you snap and kill her just like you assaulted her before that?"

Kevin heard Brett mumble denials, "I did no such thing! Why would I kill Lily? You're as mad as she is if you think I did anything to her. I didn't kill any of those women, when will someone believe me?"

The woman snorted, "I'm aware you didn't kill the other women Brett because I did. Not that it worked, the police were supposed to start investigating you both and I'd finally find out what happened to Lily. Of course, no one gave a shit about her and as it looks as though you're both going to get off scott free I decided to take matters into my own hands."

There was a pause and Kevin wondered what was going on before he heard Andrea speak again.

"What about you Piper? Did you kill her? Was it to get her out of his life or did he know what you were planning to do, even more than that did he tell you to hurt her?"

Piper's voice held a note of fear, but you had to strain to hear it, "I did nothing of the sort. Why would I kill her? Who the hell are you anyway? Lily never mentioned a sister."

The woman gave a cold chuckle, "Who am I? I'm Andrea Banks, Lily's older sister."

Not taking the situation seriously enough Piper snorted, "This is ridiculous and you know it. Instead of threatening us why aren't you trying to find out where she went and which poor sod she's stalking and harrassing now?"

Her goading didn't go down well, Andrea was angry and it radiated from every word she screamed at Piper.

"If you knew what else I've already done for her you wouldn't be brushing me off like this. Let's see how cocky you are when I start cutting bits off your boyfriend."

Greggs realised he wasn't going to get time to wait for back-up. Slipping into the room he crept closer and hid behind the sofa. He needed Andrea to be so focused on Brett that she wouldn't sense him approaching. As soon as he got an opportunity he was planning to jump her.

Brett was handcuffed to a chair in the corner of the room, his eyes fixed on the big sharp kitchen knife Andrea had in her hand. She was leaning over him, waving the blade and becoming increasingly agitated.

"What shall I chop off first? Maybe an ear or the tip of a finger, what would you rather lose? Maybe I should pop out one of your eyes?"

Brett pulled his head away from the knife that she was poking closer and closer to his face.

"Please don't! I didn't hurt Lily, I swear on my life I didn't, you've got it all wrong."

She threw back her head and laughed, "Why should I believe you?"

Piper was struggling with her cuffs and Andrea turned her attention back to her, "If it wasn't him, it had to be you. Are you going to let me cut him rather than talk?"

Andrea moved the knife from one prisoner to the other, "I killed my own parents you know. Lily was leading the life from hell so I waited until she went to a sleepover and burned the house down with them in it. They were so stoned they didn't know a thing about it until it was too late. Then social services screwed me over by not allowing her to come and live with me. It was all for nothing as they dumped her in one shitty foster home after another. She was vulnerable and she was all I had and then one of you took her from me."

Brett was looking horrified, "What do you mean you killed your parents? Are you completely mad? No wonder Lily was so fucked up."

"Don't talk about my sister like that – it was people like you that fucked her up."

Andrea bent over Brett and pulled out his hand, she splayed out his fingers and held the knife over them.

"Shall we play this little piggy to decide which one we're going to take?"

Kevin saw Piper kick out at Andrea, "Okay, okay, stop. I'll tell you what happened."

Andrea turned to her, "I'll know if you're lying."

Piper nodded, "You're right, I killed her. I used Brett's phone to message her so she thought it was him she was meeting. I deleted the message so Brett wouldn't find out and arranged to see her at his Aunty

Beryl's place. When I showed up instead she went to leave but I held her arm and made her listen to me. I told her to leave him alone and back off but she just laughed in my face. When I told her we'd take out an injunction against her she stopped laughing and told me if she couldn't have him no one would. I knew she'd end up killing him and I couldn't let that happen. We all know the police wouldn't have any teeth either. I picked up a brick and smashed it into her face. I had to hit her another three times before I knew she was dead. I buried her on Beryl's land and that's where she'll still be."

There was a stunned silence before Piper spoke again, "I'm not sorry, I had no choice. The accusations of assault she made against Brett were just the start, and I knew she'd never stop. I didn't screw her up and neither did Brett, but we were supposed to put up with the fall out from her madness."

Kevin closed his eyes for a moment, this wasn't going to end well. Why the hell was Piper goading a woman with a knife? Backup wasn't going to make it in time and Andrea was already moving towards Piper with a look of determination and hatred. If he didn't move now, Piper was going to die and whilst he thought she was a despisable creature it was his job to make sure she faced the legal concequences for her actions.

Crouching he put his weight onto the balls of his feet. Taking a deep breath he sprang forward, arms outstretched toward Andrea hoping against hope she didn't get to stick that knife in him before he made contact.

His arms closed around her and he automatically twisted his body away from her knife hand. Andrea gave a howl of rage, but Kevin's weight took her off her feet. It was chaos, she was lashing out and he couldn't be sure if he'd got there in time. Quickly he reached over and turned her wrist over until she cried out in pain and dropped the knife.

"Get the fuck off me!"

Kevin pushed down harder trying to keep his grip on her as she wriggled and bucked to try and get away.

Hearing Steve's footsteps, he didn't take his eyes off her as he called over to him, "Give me a hand restraining this wild cat Harding. And I hope you've called for backup."

It wasn't until he saw the blood that Kevin realised Andrea had managed to slice his arm with the knife. He winced as the paramedic cleaned and dressed it.

"I'd suggest you go to the hospital to check if it needs stitches, but I get the impression you're not the sort of guy who'd take my advice."

Kevin shrugged and then winced when the movement pulled his wound, "You've got me spot on. I'm not planning on going anywhere until I know that woman is fit for me to interview."

The paramedic glanced over in her direction, Andrea was handcuffed and being spoken to by his colleague. Her face was a mask of pure rage and from her pursed lips she wasn't responding to anything being said to her.

"Pete's great with the mental health stuff, he'll get to the bottom of what's going on with her."

There was silence while Kevin watched as a stretcher was wheeled out of the room, from the lack of urgency he knew it meant Piper hadn't made it.

Andrea must've managed to stab her just before Kevin made contact with her.

Sitting on the sofa was Brett, his head in his hand he wept quietly as one of the female PCs patted him ineffectually on the shoulder. Kevin bit back a grin, Yvonne was quite possibly the last person he'd ask to offer comfort to anyone. She was a nice woman but tended to be quite blunt and forthright.

Yvonne flashed him a look that suggested she'd reached the height of her patience meter with the crying Brett. He was about to go over when Harding caught his eye.

"I'll take this one boss, you save your strength for all that lovely paperwork we'll need to complete later."

Chapter Fourteen

Beryl Stratford had been incandescent with rage when they'd showed up at her house with a search warrant and started digging up her gardens. She'd pulled on her welly boots and positioned herself on the patio where she could stand and watch everything they were doing.

When it got chilly and dark Beryl fetched out a blanket and a large vodka and tonic. Sitting on the wooden chair that matched the big expensive outdoor table she glared at them. Everything annoyed her, but she really went ballistic when they bought the floodlights in so they could work through the night.

"What in God's name are you doing? Everyone from here to the other side of town will know what's going on. You may not give a shit about my good name, but it's all I have left."

Kevin couldn't find any pity for her. She'd raised Brett to be the way he'd turned out and she'd encouraged Piper's strange obsession that had led to Lily's death. If Piper hadn't been so desperate to protect Brett she'd never have killed that poor woman.

When they'd found Lily's decomposed remains she'd fallen silent. It seemed she wasn't entirely heartless when on hearing there was no one to bury her she'd stumped up the money to pay for her funeral.

"I can't have the poor kid being dumped in a pauper's grave. It wouldn't be right. Brett cared about her once and someone should take responsibility for her. I didn't realise she didn't have any parents, she never said, and with her sister standing trial for murder it's not as though she can help out is it?"

Beryl waved away Kevin's thanks with an impatient hand, "Don't make a big deal out of it please DCI Greggs."

It wasn't often that people surprised him. His years in the police had put him in contact with the worst society had to show for itself, but Beryl had made him reconsider making snap judgments.

Brett was madly in love with his latest flame. Fran had apparently bowed out of Brett's life when the whole Piper and Lily thing came to light, but as was the way with Brett he'd soon found himself a replacement. Kevin met her when he went over to update Brett on the case. Leona wasn't his usual type, in fact, he'd say she was more like Piper which was disturbing. She seemed to have the measure of Brett as she brusquely told him that everything would be fine.

"Wherever Andrea ends up she'll be away from Brett. Hospital or prison, it doesn't make any difference really does it?"

Kevin could see her point, but there was something annoying about the thought of Andrea pulling one last fast one and ending up in hospital rather than on a prison wing.

Andrea was due to be given a full psychiatric assessment in the lead-up to her trial. Kevin didn't think she was crazy, she'd been too meticulous, too well organised, but she was also smart and resourceful so he wouldn't put it passed her to fool everyone. Ethan had summed up the reasons why it felt as though the system was desperate to find a reason for what she'd done.

"I think people find it hard to believe that a woman can do evil things and they look for another explanation. They want to find something wrong with her to soothe their fears, and I imagine they'll keep looking until they decide on a label for her."

Ethan should know, thought Greggs, this was the second time he'd looked an unexpected evil in the face. He'd even carried out his own evaluation on Andrea, one that the prosecution was planning to use to try and thwart her attempts to get found unfit to stand trial.

"I can't promise it'll do any good, but I'm willing to try."

Ethan's face had taken on a serious expression, "She deserves a cell at HMP Chartridge and not a precious bed in the forensic mental health system. Hearing her tell me about her background almost made me feel sorry for her, but then I think of those women who she killed just to punish Brett and Piper and I remind myself she's a stone-cold psychopath."

Kevin knew Ethan must've been fighting with his natural urge to feel empathy, "Do you think things would've turned out differently if Lily had been placed with Andrea all those years ago?"

He'd shaken his head at the DCI, "I doubt it, the rot would've already set in by then. Don't forget, at that point she'd killed her parents just to get Lily to live with her. She told me all about that too. How she'd snuck into the house and watched them sleep for long enough to know they were out for the count before lighting one of her parent's cigarettes and leaving it to catch light to the curtains."

Ethan had shuddered, "She stood outside watching the house burn and making sure neither of them escaped. That's cold, no matter what they did it's not usual for anyone to be able to kill their own family like that. The only time I saw any emotion from Andrea was when she showed her anger and disgust for a system that she feels is responsible for tearing her and Lily apart."

"Did the sisters have any contact over the years?"

The doctor nodded, "Lily regularly met up with Andrea who encouraged her to sabotage her placements to get to live with her. According to Andrea, Lily had decided to move in just before Piper killed her. She saw Piper's actions as being yet another, final, way of stopping them from being together."

Kevin swung his legs up onto the sofa and leaned back into the soft cushions. He was exhausted, he'd given his all for this. Not only that but he'd put his reputation on the line. He might have got it wrong about Brett, but he'd said all along those deaths weren't an accident.

Earlier in the day he'd had a brief conversation with Jose Melian. The Guardia Civil officer listened in silence to the whole story.

"So, your gut feeling was right all along. People dismiss us too easily I find. Well done, and if you're ever visiting my island let me know and we'll go for a beer to celebrate."

Kevin smiled as he hung up the phone, he might just do that, he thought. He'd enjoyed his short break in Tenerife and it'd be nice to go back without the weight of the case on his shoulders.

As his eyes drifted closed, he felt the tension ease in his shoulders. The cut on his arm was healing well but it itched like a fucker. Every time it flared up it reminded him of the close call with Andrea. It would be a permanent reminder too, as the doctor he'd finally seen had told him it was likely to leave a scar.

Considering the alternative he felt he'd got off lightly. Not only that but Brett hadn't been left with so much as a scratch. If nothing else he could congratulate himself on that alone. Not that Brett had said so much as a thank you to him. Kevin didn't care, he'd done his job and made sure the right person had paid. He'd found Lily too, the poor young woman who'd been through so much had finally been laid to rest.

Kevin hadn't thought anyone would go to Lily's funeral, however he'd been surprised to see Beryl at the front of the room. It wasn't just her either, even Brett had shown up, and most surprising of all, Misty Groves. She'd come alone and spent the brief service dabbing her eyes with a large white hanky. Afterwards, she'd shaken Kevin's hand.

"Thank you for letting me know what happened to Lily. I had to come and say a final goodbye. She left me so quickly I didn't really get a chance and it didn't feel right not to do so now."

Kevin allowed himself a moment to wonder if things might have got better for Lily if Piper hadn't killed her when she did. He liked to think so, but then he could be a bit of an optimist at times.

Piper's funeral had been far less well attended, Brett's new girlfriend had stopped him from going, Aunty Beryl hadn't wanted to after discovering Piper had buried Lily in her garden, and apparently her family didn't want to be connected with what she'd done. In the end, it was just him, Ethan, and DS Potter who'd stood around the grave as she was lowered in.

Kevin's team had talked about going to the pub and toasting their success, but he just hadn't felt up to it. Maybe it was age catching up on him, or maybe he was just on the verge of burnout, but the idea of getting dressed up and going anywhere hadn't appealed. He'd rather stretch out on his couch, drink a tinned beer, and try and process the end of the case in the comfort of his own home. A ring on his doorbell made him cuss quietly to himself, the last thing he wanted was to get up from his comfortable spot on the sofa.

"It'd better not be cold sales," he muttered to himself irritably as he threw open the door. The scowl dropped away when he saw who it was.

Ethan and Steve didn't give him an opportunity to object as they marched into his house carrying a pack of beer each.

Ethan turned to him with a grin, "If the DCI won't come to the celebration, then the celebration will come to the DCI."

Kevin rolled his eyes, "Ethan, you're so witty."

Kevin felt the tiredness lift as he pointed them in the direction of his fridge, "I've got some cold ones in there so we can make a start on those while these cool down."

Watching the pair of them bickering good-naturedly about football as they made their way to the kitchen he smiled.

Life wasn't all bad, he decided.

Printed in Great Britain
by Amazon

39859672R00099